MURDER MAKES MUSIC

An Amy Bell Mystery

D1550588

DAVID SCHWINGER

PAGE PUBLISHING, INC.
New York, NY

First originally published by Page Publishing, Inc. 2019

Although some named locations, such as City College, are real, all depictions of persons, events, and policies at any and all locations in this book are intended to be completely fictional.

ISBN 978-1-64584-092-3 (Paperback)
ISBN 978-1-64584-093-0 (Digital)

Printed in the United States of America

Also by David Schwinger

The Teacher's Pet Murders

Murder Spoils the Perfect Romance

Murder with Magic

Murder Takes the Top Prize

Murder on the Lido Deck

Letter-Perfect Murder

Willing to Murder

Retirement Was Murder

Reputation for Murder

Murder Couldn't Wait

To all the people who hear me sing and are kind enough to smile pleasantly and not tell me to please shut up

Friday, July 8, 2016

Filip Beron sat at a desk in the modest one-story building which was the corporate headquarters of Acme Melodies, in Woodside, Queens, New York. Filip smiled as he pondered his good fortune.

It was after seven in the evening, and everyone else had gone home. But Filip enjoyed being alone in the office of the man who had changed his life forever. That man had provided Filip with a spare key so that he could lock up the building when he left. Sometimes, on an occasional Friday, Filip even stayed at the office overnight, slept on the sofa, and didn't head home until midday Saturday.

In spring 2014, Filip had been a twenty-seven-year-old low-level postal employee in Sofia, Bulgaria, living alone in a dingy two-room apartment.

He had not gone to university and had no serious prospects of advancement or of getting a better job elsewhere. His relationships with women had all ended after several months at the most, and he knew it was mainly his own fault.

Filip had, for many years, enjoyed composing songs, both words and music. He had no formal training, and when he sang his songs for friends and relatives, they responded kindly but not enthusiastically. However, Filip enjoyed listening to himself singing, and that brightened up his otherwise dull life.

His song lyrics were usually written in Bulgarian, but he had a modest knowledge of English and sometimes wrote in that language for his nonexistent international audience.

Filip had made a CD recording of him singing nine of his English-language songs, and he sent copies of the CD to twenty music companies in the United States and England. He received no response whatsoever from nineteen of them.

But Morton Glassberg, the president of Acme Melodies, did respond. Morton absolutely loved one of Filip's songs, entitled "I'll Never Believe It." Morton also raved about Filip's singing voice and said he would help Filip come to America to professionally record and perform this and other songs.

Filip initially assumed that this was some kind of scam, but as it turned out, Morton was on the up-and-up. The faith that Acme's president had in Filip's song and singing voice was vindicated, beyond Filip's wildest dreams. With the help of a top-notch arranger, and with Morton's assistant somewhat modifying the lyrics, "I'll Never Believe It" became a smash hit, and Filip obtained many bookings to perform in various US cities. He now lived in a four-room apartment in Forest Hills, in a luxury building with lots of amenities, and he had a second hit single, "It's Not in My Power," which had been released in March of the current year.

Sexy young women—usually teenagers—waited after his shows to get his autograph and, in some cases, to try to get something more from Filip.

Filip was relaxing in a comfortable cushioned chair on the visitor's side of Morton Glassberg's impressive desk, occasionally glancing at the photos on the wall of music celebrities posing with the man who had given Filip his big break and made him something of a star. On a page in a loose-leaf notebook, he was writing some possible lyrics to go with a melody he had recently composed.

But Filip Beron was blissfully unaware that this would be his last musical composition, and an unfinished one at that. There was a second person, who had recently stepped into the Acme Melodies headquarters building and who had quietly entered Morton's office through the open door. This person approached Filip from behind, removed a handgun from a shopping bag, blurted out a few very unpleasant words, and then fired four shots at Filip at close range before departing unobserved by human or camera.

The killer thought that Filip had died instantly. However, although mortally wounded, Filip was able to write four letters onto his loose-leaf page before he died.

Within a few days, the police had arrested a suspect in Filip's murder. But it took a perceptive private detective—who loved "I'll Never Believe It"—to identify the real killer and bring that culprit to justice.

Wednesday, August 3, 2016, afternoon

At 2:15 p.m., Amy Bell was sitting in her office at Spy4U Services Inc., where she was vice president for sensitive investigations. She was still basking in a feeling of pride and exhilaration with regard to the events of the previous week in Philadelphia, where history had been made.

She looked down at her blouse to confirm that she was indeed wearing her blue "I'm with Her, Hillary 2016" button. It was important for Amy to show solidarity with the first woman presidential nominee of a major party, and—as the Republicans had nominated Donald Trump a few days prior to the Philadelphia Democratic Party convention—beyond a doubt, the next president of the United States.

Amy's family had a long tradition of "progressive" political liberalism, and Amy had preserved that tradition, although it had become tarnished by something she never would have dreamed could happen until it did occur—namely, Jeremy Green.

She had first met Jeremy at Marty's, an East Side singles bar, on a Friday evening in March 2007, when she was twenty-one years old and Jeremy was three years older. Amy was immediately struck by Jeremy's classical good looks, wavy brown hair, and hazel eyes. At five foot eleven, he was seven inches taller than her.

Amy left her best friend Cathy at the table where they had been sitting and led Jeremy upstairs to a quieter table for two. He was rather shy, but their conversation went well until she asked him what twentieth-century figure he most admired. Jeremy responded by naming Ronald Reagan, and Amy was not pleased, to say the least.

In the political debate that followed, Amy called Jeremy some choice names such as "reactionary" and "self-hating Jew." But she remained very attracted to him and planned to ask him to return with her to the apartment she shared with Cathy. However, when she left the table to get her coat, Jeremy departed Marty's through a back door and went home. He had decided that the very attractive City College senior and political science major with whom he had been talking was a nutcase and hated his guts to boot.

Luckily, Eddie Mitchell—with whom Jeremy had gone to Marty's and who had hit it off with Cathy, whom he eventually married—persuaded his friend to give Amy a second chance. Jeremy phoned Amy the next day, and that was the start of a torrid affair which lasted a couple of months. Amy and Jeremy then agreed to date other people while still being friends with benefits. Finally, two and a half years later, they realized they had loved each other all along, and they married in January 2010.

When people asked Amy how she could have married a conservative like Jeremy—whom Amy usually called Jerry—she often responded that sometimes life smacks you in the ass and screws up everything. But politics aside, Jeremy meant everything to Amy, and she was always aware of how lucky she was that her ass had been smacked.

Jeremy was a freelance actuary who usually worked out of their two-bedroom, two-bath co-op apartment in Greenwich Village. In addition, he often assisted his wife with her tough detective cases. Amy felt that there were several murder cases she probably would not have solved without Jeremy's input.

Amy's contemplations regarding Hillary and Jeremy were interrupted by the ringing of her office phone. It was Chester Murray, the founder and president of Spy4U. Chester had hired Amy part-time in August 2003 and full-time upon her graduation from CCNY. A few years later, Amy solved the murder of three students in an adult education class she was taking and became, for a while, a minor celebrity. To avoid losing her, Chester promoted Amy to her current VP title, a decision he never regretted. In the years since then, Amy had become a star at Spy4U, and in addition to supervising several subordinates, she had solved numerous difficult cases, including more than ten murders.

"Hi, Amy, can you come to my office now? There's a man here whom you may recognize from a previous murder investigation, and he wants to hire you regarding another murder."

"Sure, Mr. Murray, I'll be there in two minutes. Who's the man?"

"I won't tell you; see if you can identify him."

Intrigued, Amy proceeded down the hall and entered Chester's office. Sitting next to Chester was a gray-haired man, dressed impeccably in a dark-brown suit, who appeared to be about sixty years old. He smiled broadly at Amy.

"Hello, Amy, do you remember me?"

"Of course! You're Steven Atwood, and you received three million dollars as one of the lucky beneficiaries in a will."

Steven laughed. "Yep, you've got me dead to rights!"

Chester provided wine for everyone, and after various pleasantries, Steven got to the point. "Amy, in the previous case, where we first met, you solved a murder that I am positive no one else would ever have been able to solve."

Amy blushed. "Aw, shucks!"

Steven laughed. "I really believe that. You are one in a million. But anyhow, I want to tell you about Anthony Capadora—everyone calls him Tony. He's the son of two good friends of mine, who are both, unfortunately, now deceased. Tony is thirty-five years old, and I've known him since he was a young boy.

"In all the years that I've known Tony, he has been a highly ethical, God-fearing person. Tony attends my church. He teaches high-school history, and he volunteers his time for several charities.

"Tony is single, and he lives alone in a rented one-bedroom bungalow in Elmhurst. He's had a few girlfriends, and those relationships all eventually ended amicably.

"On July 15 of this year, Tony was arrested for first-degree murder. I am one hundred percent certain that Tony is totally innocent. As the caring, decent person I know him to be, he is simply incapable of committing such a crime."

"Steven," interrupted Amy, "who has Tony allegedly murdered?"

"Filip Beron, a singer, originally from Bulgaria and now residing in Forest Hills."

"Oh, my god! Do you mean the Filip Beron who sang 'I'll Never Believe It?' I love that song!"

Steven nodded. "Yeah, that's him. I was doing very well, financially, for many years before receiving that three million, and I've decided that the best thing I can do now with some of my money is use it to try to exonerate Tony.

"I paid Tony's bail; he has to remain in New York City and wear a monitoring device. I also hired a first-rate criminal lawyer, Mark Traybert, to defend him. Mark has told me he's not optimistic. Amy, I want to hire you and Spy4U to try to prove Tony's innocence."

"Why is the lawyer pessimistic? What's the evidence against Tony?"

Steven nodded. "I'm very familiar with the case, and I'll lay it out for you. Tony writes songs as a hobby. About a year ago, he attended a live performance by Filip Beron. Tony waited after the show to speak to Filip and then asked him if he would be willing to listen to some of Tony's song compositions and, if he liked them, maybe he could record one of Tony's songs for his next CD.

"Filip suggested that Tony come to the Woodside headquarters of Acme Melodies, Filip's record company, and he would listen to Tony's songs. They agreed on a date and a meeting time of seven in the evening. Filip told Tony that he did most of his best songwriting at Acme's office, after everyone else had left for the day.

"Tony had not recorded any of his songs, nor could he write musical notation or play music. So Filip agreed to listen to Tony sing his songs live and *a cappella*. Tony arrived for his appointment and sang eight songs for Filip, who then thanked Tony for coming but told him that, regretfully, he couldn't use any of the songs.

"Then, about eight months later, Acme Melodies released Filip singing 'It's Not in My Power,' and it immediately became a hit. When Tony heard it, he realized that Filip had stolen the melody, note for note, as well as many of the words, from one of the songs he had sung for Filip at the Acme office.

"Tony went back to Acme to complain, but he had no evidence to support his claim, so the company president refused to get involved, and when Tony saw Filip there, the singer brushed him off.

"So Tony went to the media. Some local newspapers published articles about the dispute. Tony managed to obtain one TV interview, as well as two on the radio. He also went to see several lawyers, all of whom said that, without corroborating evidence, he did not have a case."

Amy was confused. "That wouldn't even be close to enough evidence to charge Tony with murder."

"You're right, Amy, but that's just the beginning. On Friday, July 8, Filip stayed after hours at the Acme office. Several employees at Acme confirmed that Filip was sitting in the office of Morton Glassberg, Acme's president, when they left at five p.m. Morton was aware of where Filip liked to sit after hours, and he had happily approved of this and provided Filip with a spare key to lock up the building when he left. I've been led to understand that sometimes, if he was composing late into a Friday evening, Filip slept overnight at the Acme office, continued composing on Saturday morning, and finally went home at around noon.

"Anyhow, back to Filip's murder. The building usually had no activity on weekends—except when Filip was there—and when people arrived for work on the following Monday morning, they found the building's front door unlocked and Filip's dead body in Morton's office. He had clearly been shot. They called 911. The police removed the body, and it was later determined that Filip had been shot four times, in the back of the head, neck, and shoulder. Given the delay, the time of death could only be estimated as between five o'clock on Friday evening and noon on Saturday.

"The police collected a loose-leaf notebook from the floor near the body, as well as a pen. Both had Filip's fingerprints on them. All the handwriting in the loose-leaf was identified as Filip's. The final entry, on the last page with writing on it, was the four capital letters *CAPA*. The final *A* tailed off at the end, which would be consistent with Filip dying just after writing that letter. The police provided me with a photocopy of that final loose-leaf page. Would you like to see it?"

Amy nodded. "Sure." Steven opened his briefcase, produced a sheet of paper, and handed it to Amy, who perused the photocopy as Steven continued, also looking, over Amy's shoulder, at the sheet in her hand.

"It appears to be lyrics for a new song, all in capital letters. 'I've loved you from the start. With my whole entire heart. Let's never be apart.' And then, sloping down, across several lines on the page, the large letters *CAPA*, with the final *A* sloping down even more than the other letters. It does all look like the same person's handwriting, and it looks like a kind of dying declaration."

Amy nodded. "Yes, it does. And the lyrics Filip was writing aren't very creative."

Steven laughed. "That's an understatement. Luckily, companies like Acme have people who can improve the lyrics if the melody makes it worthwhile.

"Amy, you can keep the photocopy. I have others. Anyhow, it soon became known that those four letters, *CAPA*, were the first four letters of Tony's last name and that Tony had accused Filip of stealing his song. The police obtained a warrant to search Tony's bungalow. In the backyard, they observed an area which had clearly recently been dug up and then refilled. They dug down and found a handgun, in a clear plastic bag. The gun was later determined to be the murder weapon. The gun was untraceable; the killer undoubtedly had obtained it illegally."

Amy interrupted again. "Were there any fingerprints or any DNA on the gun, or possibly on the plastic bag or on any bullets still in the gun?"

"Good question. No DNA. With regard to fingerprints, Mark, Tony's lawyer, informed me that the police often can't get any good fingerprints off a gun. On the other hand, there are some new, sophisticated methods to obtain fingerprints from a gun, even if the killer thinks he had wiped them off. Also, there are now tests to determine, with a high degree of accuracy, the gender of the person who left the prints.

"In this case, there were two good prints on the gun, one very likely from a male and one from a female. Neither of the two prints was from Tony, and the prints were not found in any database. But the police are assuming that Tony acquired the gun illegally and the prints were from past users, prior to his acquisition.

"And there was nothing on any bullets or on the plastic bag. I actually did ask; the police were very thorough in that regard."

Amy nodded. "It does look very bad for Tony. I assume he has no convincing alibi for the time frame when the killing could have occurred."

"Right. No alibi for most of that period."

"Steven, before making any final commitment to take the case, I have to speak to Tony. He will have to take and pass a polygraph test."

Chester laughed. "Steven, I told you Amy would say that."

Steven smiled. "Of course, you have to meet with Tony first. I'm absolutely certain he will agree to take a polygraph, and he will pass with flying colors. Chester, let's you and I go over all the bureaucratic details and get something signed, to take effect if and when Amy officially accepts the case. Is that OK with you, Amy?"

Amy nodded. "Sure, great idea. I'll get back to my office and do some work on my other cases. It was a pleasure seeing you again, Steven." They shook hands, and Amy departed.

As soon as she got back to her office, Amy phoned her husband, who was, as usual, at home, doing actuarial work on his computer. "Jerry, Jerry! I will probably be investigating a new murder case! I'll give you the details when I get home, after dinner."

"Wow, sweetheart, murder cases really do turn you on! What should I pick up for dinner?"

"How about a large pepperoni pizza with mushrooms; we can split it. And to celebrate, also pick up a chocolate cake from Adamo's Bakery. Then I'll tell you about the new case. After that, I'll have my way with your entire sexy body. And I plan to take my own good time on that last activity."

Before Jeremy could respond, Amy hung up the phone.

Wednesday, August 3, 2016, evening

As he watched his wife eat their dinner pizza, Jeremy Green observed her long black hair, her piercing brown eyes, and her shapely, filled-out figure. He had been very hot for Amy ever since their earlier phone conversation, and now he was even hotter. But he knew he'd have to wait until they had dissected Amy's newest murder case.

After the cake had been eaten, Amy presented to her husband what Steven had told her. "So, Jerry, what are your first impressions? Of course, we're assuming that Tony will pass the polygraph."

Jeremy was contemplative. "I think the two major pieces of evidence against Tony can be easily explained. First we have the dying letters, *CAPA*. Filip may not have known who just shot him, but he still wanted to let the police know that his likely killer was Tony Capadora, who had this gigantic grudge against him. So he started writing the name 'Capadora' in the loose-leaf, but he died after writing the first four letters.

"Second, we have the gun buried in Tony's backyard. If the killer knew about Tony's claim against Filip, he or she would know that Tony would be a prime suspect and that the police would probably search Tony's property, looking for the mur-

MURDER MAKES MUSIC

der weapon. So the killer buried the gun in a clumsy, easily detectable way, in Tony's backyard, possibly in the middle of the night, when no one would likely notice."

Amy nodded. "I had thought of those explanations, and I'm very impressed that you did too." She stroked her husband's cheek and flashed him a sly smile. "Jerry, you are a very smart boy, and you will soon be rewarded for being so smart." Amy observed a growing bulge under her husband's pants.

Jerry decided that it would be best for him to just continue discussing his impressions. "Also, I suggest you ask Tony to sing for you what he feels are several of his best other songs. See if any of them are as good as 'It's Not in My Power' or are at least reasonably good songs. If none of them is any good, you can assume that Tony did not write 'It's Not in My Power.' Boy, I really am smart!"

Amy again started stroking Jeremy's cheek. "Bad boy! Now you're too overconfident about how smart you are. I don't have to ask Tony to sing any of his songs. All I have to do is have Franklin Sorel, my polygraph guy, ask Tony if he wrote all the music and many of the words for Filip's song, 'It's Not in My Power.' Franklin is the best polygraph man on the East Coast, so after he gives us his report, we'll know the truth about the song."

Amy continued stroking her husband's cheek as she reached down with her other hand and entered it into his pants. "Now, don't you feel like a silly boy?"

At this point, Jeremy was in no condition to continue the discussion. He grabbed Amy's rear end and directed her toward

21

their master bedroom, where Amy did, indeed, as promised, take her own good time having her way with Jeremy's entire body before providing him with the maximum reward for being a smart boy.

Eventually, the couple exited the bedroom and continued their conversation regarding the case. "Sweetheart," began Jeremy, "are there any other logical suspects? After all, if Tony didn't kill Filip, then somebody else did."

Amy shook her head. "I haven't yet begun the investigation, but offhand, there's no other obvious suspects. There could be an angry girlfriend, or a former girlfriend, who felt that Filip had seriously mistreated her. There could be a groupie fan whom Filip had rejected when she propositioned him. Or maybe Filip had sex with the groupie and she now regrets it and feels angry and bitter."

Jeremy laughed. "All the possible suspects you just mentioned are female. Any possible male suspects?"

"Well, maybe Filip had somehow offended an employee at Acme. That employee would know all about Filip staying after hours at the office, where the singer would be all alone. And of course, now that Filip had money, we'll have to find out who inherits, which could conceivably be a motive for murder. Or even the parent of a groupie, who found out that Filip had sex with his or her underage daughter and was enraged. Or maybe some guy who was angry that Filip stole his girlfriend. Of course, now I'm just reaching for anything, no matter how unlikely."

"So, sweetheart, I assume your first step is to speak to Tony and get him to take the polygraph."

Amy nodded. "Right. Then I want to speak to Morton Glassberg, the president of Acme Melodies, who realized Filip's talent when he sent Acme a CD of his music and who brought Filip here from Bulgaria. Filip's rags-to-riches story has been pretty well publicized; I remember reading about it in a magazine. Anyhow, Morton probably knew Filip better than anyone else, and maybe he also knows of some other people who had a reason to want Filip dead."

Thursday, August 4, 2016

At ten thirty in the morning, Amy Bell picked up her office phone and called Franklin Sorel. She had used his polygraph services many times before, and Franklin immediately recognized her voice.

"Amy, what a joy to hear from you again. And just in the nick of time! My wife was so pleased with the first piece of alexandrite jewelry I recently bought her that she wants to acquire an alexandrite collection. And the polygraph fees I've received from you and your wonderful company have been so helpful to me in paying for her jewelry."

"Well, Franklin, you know how badly I want your wife to be happy. I will probably have a polygraph for you to do, as soon as possible. A man has been charged with first-degree murder, and there's a good chance that he's totally innocent. Also, he claims the dead man stole his song, which I have to verify."

"Fantastic! I'll rearrange my schedule for you and jack up the fee! Murder plus song theft, this should be interesting."

Amy provided Franklin with the questions she wanted him to ask and told him she'd probably contact him later in the day to set up a time for the test. At eleven fifteen, she left her office and took the subway to Elmhurst.

At twelve ten, Tony Capadora managed a smile as he ushered Amy into his small detached bungalow. He offered Amy a drink; she accepted a Diet Pepsi. They took seats in the living room.

"Amy—may I call you Amy?"

"Of course, Tony."

"Amy, I'm so grateful that you are considering taking on my case. Steven told me you require that I take a polygraph. Of course, I'll do that whenever you can set it up."

"I'm glad to hear that. My polygraph man, Franklin Sorel, is located in Midtown Manhattan. He will ask you whether you killed Filip Beron and whether you have any knowledge regarding who killed him. He will also ask whether you wrote the music and many of the words to 'It's Not in My Power.' I assume that's OK with you."

"Fine with me. The answers are no, no, and yes. And, Amy, I'm absolutely terrified. I've been set up for a murder I had nothing to do with. I'm out on bail, and I have to wear a monitoring device. I can't leave the city of New York. My trial is scheduled for mid-October. And if it wasn't for Steven, I would have no chance at all. Thank God for Steven."

Amy nodded. "You're sure as hell right about that. What's your explanation for the letters *CAPA* written by Filip just before he died?"

"I found out about those four letters when they did a story about the murder on an evening TV news show the Monday that they found the body. Someone involved with the police had leaked it to the media; my lawyer told me they were not supposed to reveal that kind of information publicly.

"Anyhow, I first assumed that the killer probably wrote those letters down after Filip had been shot, in an effort to frame me. But then I was told that Filip definitely wrote those letters. So the only explanation is that Filip didn't know who shot him, but due to my saying that he stole my song, he assumed it was me, and that's why he started to write my name."

"What about the gun in your backyard?"

"Well, the police didn't search my house until that Thursday—I was arrested on Friday—so the killer had plenty of time to go to my house and bury the gun in my backyard. I was teaching summer school in the mornings, so I was not home at that time, and the place where the gun was found would not be visible to passersby or neighbors. And I was the obvious patsy to frame, as my claim of song theft had been publicized in the media and the letters *CAPA* in Filip's loose-leaf had been revealed publicly on TV."

"Who do you think may have killed Filip?"

"I have no idea, but if Filip was such a lowlife that he would steal my song, he probably made lots of enemies who would've liked to see him dead."

"But you have no evidence that you wrote 'It's Not in My Power,' do you?"

"No. I didn't retain any written records, and I never made a recording. I should have been suspicious when Filip asked me if I had sung my songs to anyone else. The answer was no. Truth is, I was kind of embarrassed about my songs. I had no self-confidence; I thought my songs would be thought of by other people as all being lousy.

"But for some reason, having listened to Filip's big hit song, 'I'll Never Believe It,' and knowing his rags-to-riches story, I thought Filip might like my songs and possibly want to record and perform one or two of them. So I went to see his performance at the Astoria Showplace and waited to meet him afterwards. He seemed interested and told me to sing my songs for him at the Acme office at seven p.m. a few days later.

"Now I know why he selected that time and place. He chose a time and location when no one else would hear me sing my songs and where it would be very easy for him to secretly and clearly record me singing. Of course, I was a complete fool not to protect myself, but that's now the least of my problems."

"Tony, I've listened to Filip's recording of 'It's Not in My Power,' and I can tell you that if you composed the music and many of the words, you are a very talented songwriter. The song has been a hit, so I'm obviously not the only person with that opinion. Now let's set up the polygraph test."

Amy arrived home at five forty and was immediately shocked and horrified by what she saw. Jeremy greeted his wife at the door, wearing a big smile and a red "Make America Great Again" cap. Donald Trump had been Jeremy's second choice—behind Wisconsin governor Walker—for the Republican presidential nomination, but now, he was all in for Trump.

Jeremy was not as interested in politics as his wife, and Amy realized that her husband acquiring the cap was his revenge for Amy wearing the "I'm with Her" button. He was trying to get a rise out of her. Amy did not take the bait. She remained calm.

"Jerry, that hat should read, 'Make the Dems Control Congress and the White House Again.' Trump's nomination not only guarantees a Hillary victory in November, but he also ensures that the Democrats will regain control of both the House and the Senate. A majority of Americans despise Trump. I certainly do, and you should too, given everything you've heard him say in the past year."

Her husband smiled. "Some people may, indeed, hate Trump, but Trump loves those people, as well as all other Americans. He has sacrificed the wonderful life he previously had to try to become president, so he can improve the life of every American by cutting taxes and regulations, so as to create jobs."

"What?" Amy had given up her pretense of being calm. She was clearly now agitated. "You can't be serious! Trump wants to be president solely for his own self-aggrandizement. The only people Trump loves are rich people and, most of all, himself!"

Jeremy decided he'd had enough fun politically baiting his wife. "OK, sweetheart, let's make a deal. No buttons or caps in our apartment. I'll soak up Trump's love, and you can soak up Hillary's love." Hearing himself say this, Jeremy couldn't control himself, and he burst out laughing. He squeezed his wife and kissed her passionately. Amy responded in kind, as she thought to herself, *There's life, smacking me in the ass again.*

"OK, Jerry, deal."

After dinner, as they were cuddling with each other in the living room, watching TV, Amy's phone rang. "Hi, Amy, it's Franklin. I did Tony Capadora's polygraph, and I am very confident that Tony had no connection whatsoever with the murder of Filip Beron and that Tony did, indeed, compose the music and most of the lyrics to the song 'It's Not in My Power.' As always, I appreciate your business."

Amy nodded. "Thanks, Franklin, that's what I had expected. Send my best regards to your wife."

"Will do."

Amy hung up and smiled broadly at Jeremy. "Game on!"

Monday, August 8, 2016, a.m.

At eleven in the morning, Morton Glassberg shook Amy's hand and ushered her into his office at Acme Melodies. He sat at his desk, and Amy sat in a comfortable chair on the other side of the desk, facing Morton. They agreed to use first names.

"Amy, you are sitting in the same chair, and in the same place in the office, where Filip was sitting when he was shot."

Amy turned her neck to look back at the office entrance door. "So if the office door was open, as it probably was at that hour, and if the killer was quiet, Filip may well have been unaware that the killer had entered the office."

Morton nodded. "That could easily be true. Of course, the killer could have made some noise or possibly said something to Filip. Or maybe after being shot, Filip was able to turn and catch a glimpse of the killer. After all, he stayed alive after the four shots, long enough to write some letters in his loose-leaf."

"Of course," observed Amy, "Filip and the killer may have made an appointment to meet at that hour. I take it there is no video surveillance either outside or inside the building?"

"Sadly, no. But we're certainly gonna install video now. We're currently in the process of finalizing our plans in that regard."

Amy smiled. "Yeah, I would imagine that's what you would be doing. Tell me about how you made Filip a star."

"Well, a bit more than two years ago, I received a package, sent by Filip from Bulgaria, containing a CD with Filip singing nine songs he composed. No musical instruments, just Filip. He also enclosed some information about himself as well as a photo. I was immediately intrigued because I had never previously met anyone, or received any mail, from Bulgaria.

"When I receive submissions by mail, I am always skeptical. That kind of thing almost never results in our company producing any music. And for eight of the nine songs, my skepticism was clearly vindicated. Their melodies were mediocre, and that's being kind. Their words also left a lot to be desired.

"On the other hand, the ninth song, 'I'll Never Believe It,' struck a chord with me—pardon the pun. I felt that the melody was surprisingly catchy. The words needed some improvement, but we have people at Acme who can modify the lyrics without changing their general meaning. And of course, we have arrangers and musicians we can call upon to help Filip professionally record his song.

"I liked Filip's voice. He put excellent emotion into his singing, giving the listener the impression that Filip was expressing his deep feelings. To top it off, Filip was a very good-looking guy. Also, his life story of being a postal employee in Bulgaria could appeal to the public.

"I helped Filip come to this country and record 'I'll Never Believe It,' as a single and as part of a music video, as well as record a CD containing Filip singing that song plus several others not composed by him.

"The song became a hit, and we were able to arrange for Filip to do singing performances at various venues around the country. Now Filip has another hit single, 'It's Not in My Power,' and at the time of his death, he was in demand as a performer."

Amy interrupted. "You are, of course, aware that Tony Capadora had claimed that Filip stole 'It's Not in My Power' from him."

"Yes, I was definitely following that situation closely. Filip told me that Tony had approached him after a performance in Astoria, and he had agreed to meet with Tony in Acme's building on an evening shortly afterward, where Tony would sing his songs for him. Filip said he listened to all the songs and wasn't interested in any of them. He said that was what he told Tony.

"Filip assured me that Tony did not sing any song remotely similar to 'It's Not in My Power.' Filip said he wrote that song a few months later, and he had completely forgotten about Tony until he was accused of stealing the song. Tony produced no corroborating evidence whatsoever, and a few days before he died, Filip told me he actually felt sorry for Tony, as he knew how frustrating it is to keep writing songs that no one wants to hear."

"Are there any other people you are aware of who may have had a grudge against Filip?"

"Well, there's Oscar Banks. We dropped him a few weeks after we brought in Filip. It was basically a business decision that had nothing to do with our new relationship with Filip, but Oscar took it very hard and blamed Filip for essentially pushing him out of Acme. He said Filip had virtually no talent and Acme would soon regret their decision to dump him and go with Filip"

"Did Oscar say that to Filip, directly to his face?"

"Yes, at least once, on Oscar's last day here at Acme. The two of them were about to come to blows until I personally broke it up and escorted Oscar out of the building."

"Do you know of any contact they had after that?"

"No, and Oscar has since left the music business. He is currently doing construction work."

"Anyone else?"

"Just one more, Bart Mallon. He's a contract musician with Acme. He does soundtracks for some of our recording artists. Bart had a girlfriend, Karen Maddox, and Filip moved in on her and stole Karen away from him. Filip and Karen lasted only a couple of months as a couple before they broke up, but Bart and Karen never got back together, and Bart currently has no significant other. Bart told me he'd heard that Filip did not treat Karen well. He told me a mutual acquaintance mentioned to him that Karen said Filip had hit her, and more than once."

"Oh my god," Amy interrupted. "Oh my god!"

"Of course, I only have Bart's third-hand word on that. But Bart definitely hated Filip, and he told me as much on several occasions. However, frankly, I can't believe that Bart—or Oscar, for that matter—would even dream of murdering Filip.

"And besides, it certainly looks like Tony murdered him. As I understand it, Filip, as he was dying, was able to write down the first four letters of Tony's last name. And they found the murder weapon in Tony's backyard."

Amy nodded. "Yes, it certainly looks very bad for Tony. But I'm being paid to be very thorough."

Morton nodded. "Of course, I understand completely."

"Did Filip have any other girlfriends during the time you knew him?"

"Yes, two others, and those relationships also lasted only a few months."

"Can you get me the contact information for Oscar, Bart, Karen, and also, hopefully, the other two girlfriends?"

Morton nodded again. "Yes, I can provide you with contact information for all five of them. I'll get the information for the two men from my records, and I'm almost certain I can get the information for the three girlfriends from our talent liaison, Barry Garner. I should have everything for you by tomorrow."

"I really appreciate that. Did Filip have any friends—I mean nonromantic friends—that you are aware of?"

"Yes, Barry was a good friend, his only friend that I am aware of. Barry's job was to make sure everything ran smoothly for our contracted talent. He handled all the daily details for Filip, such as arranging meetings, recording sessions, and performances. He would also accompany Filip to his shows.

"In addition, Barry handled Filip's Facebook page. As part of Acme's contract with Filip, he was not allowed to have anything to do with that page. If a fan thought he or she was corresponding with Filip, it was actually with Barry."

Amy nodded and smiled. "That's very ingenious and also very prudent on Acme's part. What about groupies? Was Filip having sex with groupies after his shows?"

"I hope not; Barry was supposed to make sure that didn't happen. But I can't guarantee anything. You can ask Barry about that. Of course, I have his contact information too; he's still employed by Acme."

"Did Filip have any friends or relatives in Bulgaria with whom he was still in contact?"

"Just one, Petar Rykov. Filip's parents died in an auto accident four years ago. He had no brothers or sisters. Petar was a coworker of Filip's at the post office in Sofia. He had helped Filip improve his English, and they had been good friends for quite a while. I have Petar's e-mail address and phone number. Filip regularly texted Petar and occasionally phoned and e-mailed him. He was planning to invite his longtime friend to visit the US, with Filip paying all of Petar's expenses."

"Do you know whether Filip had made out a will?"

"Yes, Filip made out a will a few months ago. He talked to me about it. He said he was so grateful to me for making him a star that he wanted to make me one of his beneficiaries. I told him it was a wonderful gesture, but I suggested he leave that money to charity. He agreed, and that's what he did. Other than the three charities Filip selected, who'll split around thirty thousand dollars, he also left ten thousand to Petar and five thousand to Barry."

"Those two people, plus the three charities, were the only beneficiaries?"

Morton nodded. "Correct."

"Given Filip's very successful past two years, shouldn't Filip have ended up with more than forty-five thousand dollars?"

"You know, you're right. I guess Filip was typical of people who are suddenly successful; they frequently spend their money lavishly, at least during the first few years."

"Did you ever meet Tony in person?"

"Yes, the day he came to Acme's office to complain that Filip had stolen his song. I asked him what corroborating evidence he had. He said he didn't have any. I told him that in that case, Acme could not help him. There are many people who complain, without evidence, that a celebrity has stolen their song, so Tony showing up at Acme was not particularly unusual."

Amy changed the subject. "Morton, wouldn't Filip have locked the front door right after everyone left at around five?"

"He should have. But he wasn't reliable in that regard. The building actually has a front and a back door, both requiring the same key."

"Do other Acme employees have a copy of that same spare key?"

"Yes, many. We also leave a key in the main office in case someone needs to work late. I think we're gonna have to reevaluate our whole key policy."

Amy nodded. "That sounds like a very good idea. Well, thank you for meeting with me. You know, I really love 'I'll Never Believe It,' Filip's first hit song."

Morton smiled. "You and me and a hell of lot of other people too. There's something so catchy about that tune. I'm so grateful that Filip sent his song to me. And Filip told me he sent the same CD to lots of other music people, and none of the others ever responded."

Amy nodded. "I recall reading that *Harry Potter* was rejected by twelve publishers before someone accepted it. I guess even the professionals really cannot know what is or isn't gonna be a hit with the public."

"Amy, you've got that right!" They shook hands, and Amy departed.

Monday, August 8, 2016, p.m.

At ten past three in the afternoon, Amy entered the law offices of Adams and Traybert, located near the United Nations. She shook hands with Tony's lawyer, Mark Traybert, and they took comfortable leather seats in Mark's office. Amy accepted a glass of red wine.

"So, Ms. Bell, remind me, whom are you here about?"

"Tony Capadora."

"Tony who? Let me go through my client list." Amy watched as Mark poured over his notes for about fifteen seconds. "Oh, here it is, Anthony Capadora. What's he charged with?"

"First-degree murder." Amy was getting less and less enthusiastic about Mark being Tony's defense attorney.

"And, Ms. Bell, how exactly are you connected to Tony's case?"

"Tony's longtime friend, Steven Atwood, hired me to investigate the case in an effort to help prove that Tony is innocent. And please call me Amy."

Mark had now found Tony's file, and he was glancing at it while disregarding Amy's request. "The problem, Ms. Bell, is that all the evidence shows that Tony is guilty. He was claiming, without evidence, that Filip Beron stole his song, a claim Filip categorically rejected. The murder weapon was found in his backyard. And Filip's last action before he died was to write *CAPA* onto his loose-leaf. Additionally, Tony has no alibi for most of the period when the murder could have occurred.

"I have suggested to Tony that he plead guilty to whatever deal I can get for him to avoid a life sentence. But I'm not sure I can get him any kind of deal. There's more evidence against Tony than in most murder cases."

"Mr. Traybert," inquired Amy, "how often have you seen Tony, and do you have anyone looking for exculpatory evidence, or evidence that someone else may have committed the murder?"

"Oh yes, I visited Tony, for a half hour or so, a few days after Mr. Atwood hired me to defend him. I told Tony I'd see what I could do for him. So far, there's nothing I can do for him, so I have no reason yet to visit with him again until I have something."

"What about the fact that the murder gun was buried in such a way that it would be easy for the police to see that something had recently been buried there? So it looks like the real killer wanted to frame Tony. And also there were two unidentified fingerprints on the gun."

"The gun was untraceable and had obviously been acquired illegally, probably recently. So the two prints undoubtedly were on the gun before Tony acquired it. Your idea that the killer buried the gun in such a way as to frame Tony might be an argument, except that Filip wrote the letters *CAPA* just before he died."

"Yes, but it makes sense that Filip may well have not known who shot him, from behind, but he assumed that it was Tony, due to the song dispute, and he wanted to direct the police to Tony. Also, the letters *CAPA* were leaked to the media and appeared on TV, so the killer knew exactly whom to frame for the murder."

"Ms. Bell, I deal in the real world. Do you think the jury would give any credence to your argument, or would they be over-whelmingly likely to convict Tony for first-degree murder on their first ballot?"

Amy nodded. "You make a good point, but I have some addi-tional information to provide to you. I had Franklin Sorel administer a polygraph to Tony. Mr. Sorel is one of the top polygraph administrators in the country, and he is very con-fident, based on the polygraph results, that Tony had nothing whatsoever to do with the murder of Filip Baron. He is also very confident that Tony did, in fact, compose the music and most of the lyrics of Filip's song 'It's Not in My Power.' So Tony is, in fact, innocent of the murder."

Mark smiled. "Unfortunately, polygraphs are notoriously unre-liable and are not admissible in court. I myself beat a polygraph test at a county fair some years ago."

"Mr. Traybert, a polygraph is most accurate when the subject is aware that serious consequences are at stake, particularly serious negative consequences. Also, the caliber of the polygraph exam-iner makes a big difference."

"Ms. Bell, I admire your tenacity and your dedication to helping Tony. If I were in trouble, I would very much want you on my side. But the reality is that his best hope is for me to call in a few markers at the DA's office in an effort to get them to offer Tony a plea deal.

"By the way, the police gave me a copy of the two fingerprints found on the gun. They're pretty sure one is from a male and one is from a female. The prints were found on the barrel of the gun, not on or near the trigger. Would you like me to make you a copy of the fingerprints?"

Amy nodded vigorously. "Yes, Mr. Traybert, I would like a copy, thank you. By the way, I would like to speak with someone at the NYPD about this case. Whom should I contact?"

"Call Detective Arthur Oteri, at the Woodside Precinct. I'll let him know you'll probably be requesting a meeting with him." Mark made the requested copy of the two fingerprints for Amy, then she departed.

After dinner, Amy updated her husband on the day's interviews. When she was finished, Jeremy immediately responded. "Sweetheart, Mark Traybert sounds like he took this defense-lawyer gig as a favor to Steven and plans to spend as little time and effort on Tony's case as possible. Sad to say, you are clearly Tony's only hope."

"Jerry, you're sure as hell right about that. Mark sounded to me like he was with the DA's office, rather than Tony's defense lawyer. But Mark has given me a critical tool to solve the case. I now have a copy of the two fingerprints the police found on the gun.

"Mark and the police are assuming that those prints got on the gun before the killer acquired it. But that makes sense only if Tony is the killer, which he isn't. Since someone else shot Filip, I think it's certainly possible that one of the prints on the murder weapon came from that killer. If so, all I have to do is obtain the fingerprints for each of my suspects and see whose prints match one of the two fingerprints from the gun. That individual would almost certainly be Filip's killer."

Her husband laughed. "Even better, have all your subjects take a lie detector test."

Amy was not amused. "Ha ha, you know what would happen if I asked, say, one of Filip's former girlfriends to take a polygraph. She would angrily refuse and probably tell me never to contact her again."

"But wouldn't the same thing happen if you asked her to provide a set of her fingerprints?"

Amy smiled. "In all likelihood, you're correct. But I plan to secure the suspects' prints surreptitiously. I'll talk to Eddie to get my best strategy. Oh, and before I forget, we're going to dinner with Eddie and Cathy this Saturday. Then we'll go bowling. Cathy's mother will be babysitting Aurora."

Eddie was the same Eddie Mitchell who had advised Jeremy to give Amy a second chance and phone her the day after they first met at Marty's, back in 2007. He and his wife, Cathy—who had been Amy's best girlfriend for well over a decade—lived in Astoria, Queens. Their daughter Aurora was a little over two and a half years old. Eddie was a detective in the New York City Police Department, and Amy sometimes requested his assistance with regard to her investigations. Amy and her husband viewed the Mitchells as like family.

Jeremy nodded and smiled. "Great! Sounds like fun. So, if one of your suspects left one of the prints, this may turn out to be a very easy case. Of course, there's always the slight chance that the killer is not one of your suspects or that you can't obtain a suspect's prints or that the fingerprints actually were on the gun before the killer acquired it."

Amy laughed. "I was just being hopeful about matching prints. I understand it's a lot more than a slight chance that I won't find a match. But maybe I'll get lucky."

"Sweetheart, shouldn't the police actually be getting fingerprints from all your suspects and from anyone else they can find who knew Filip?"

"I don't think they can force people to supply prints without a warrant, unless the person has committed an offense. But Mark should be looking for other suspects. He's doing nothing. I checked him out on the web, and he does have a good reputation as a defense lawyer. But in Tony's case, he's not living up to his reputation.

"I'm gonna ask Eddie what kind of item I should bring to my interviews and then try to get the suspects to touch it. As a matter of fact, I told Cathy I'd phone her, after speaking to you, to confirm our Saturday date. I'll call her now and then ask to speak to Eddie." She punched in the number, and Eddie answered.

"Hi, Eddie, it's Amy. Tell Cathy we're on for this Saturday, and as she had suggested, we'll meet at your apartment at five thirty."

"OK, Amy, will do."

"Also, Eddie, I need your assistance; it'll be very brief."

"Uh-oh!" Eddie moaned. "I know what that usually means, and it's the opposite of *brief.*"

Amy laughed. "No, this time, it's just some little pieces of information. I want to surreptitiously obtain fingerprints from some suspects whom I plan to interview. What should I bring to the interviews to try to get them to leave their fingerprints on it?"

"There are lots of surfaces that can hold prints well, but for your scenario, clear plastic is probably best. Ask the suspects to read something or look at a photo enclosed in a clear plastic sleeve. Then hand it to them to hold. Of course, you'll need a new sleeve for each suspect. And when you hold the plastic, only hold it in one of the corners."

"And then," Amy responded, "I assume any good fingerprint expert can get the prints off the plastic and determine if they match a print that I already have, right?"

"Yes, with the understanding that some removed prints aren't in good-enough condition to make such a determination, and assuming the print you already have is clear."

"OK, great! That was easy, wasn't it? Thanks, Eddie. We'll see you guys on Saturday. We're especially looking forward to seeing how much Aurora has grown since we saw her last."

Amy got off the phone, and Jeremy had a question. "Do you think it was a mistake to tell Mark that the polygraph showed Tony was telling the truth when he claimed that Filip stole his song? Doesn't that reinforce Tony's motive for murder? It's likely to make Mark more certain that Tony is guilty. And if the DA or the jury finds out, that would probably be bad for Tony. Maybe you should have just mentioned that the polygraph confirmed that Tony had nothing to do with the murder."

Amy was silent for a few seconds. "Jerry, you do have a point. But if you trust the polygraph about the song, you should also trust the polygraph about the murder. However, we know the jury will not find out about the polygraph—in court, at least."

"That makes sense, but I still don't think you should have told Mark."

Amy nodded. "Yeah, you may indeed be right, but that's now water under the bridge. However, I will think twice before I mention it to anyone else."

Jeremy changed the subject. "Morton said that Barry, the talent liaison, was supposed to keep groupies from having sex with Filip. But Barry and Filip became good friends, and Filip even put Barry in his will. Does that mean that at least in a few cases, Barry probably allowed Filip to have a quickie with a groupie?"

Amy laughed. "That's a great line you just came up with. 'A quickie with a groupie.' I hadn't realized that you were so good at turning a phrase! Yes, I suspect that Barry allowed a few exceptions to Acme's rule about groupies. I'll definitely speak to Barry about that.

"But despite the fact that I mentioned the possibility, I think it's far-fetched that a groupie may have murdered Filip. Barry never would have permitted a continuing relationship. Of course, Filip might have been able to hide such a relationship from Barry. But still it's quite a long shot."

"Are you optimistic that your suspects will be willing to speak to you?"

"That's a very good question. Of course, Barry will speak to me, but he is not currently one of my prime suspects. Needless to say, when I ask a suspect for an interview, I will not mention that he or she is a suspect. I'll find a different, hopefully believable reason for requesting their cooperation. But you're right; one or more of them may well refuse to see me."

"Whom will you try to see first?"

"I think I'll talk to Detective Oteri of the NYPD. I'd like to know if Filip's murder is still being investigated or if they have already congratulated themselves and shut the case down.

"And I love that phrase of yours. 'A quickie with a groupie.' I think it's now time for a not-so-quickie with a hubby!" She led Jeremy to the bedroom.

Thursday, August 11, 2016

At ten thirty in the morning, Amy Bell and Detective Arthur Oteri of the NYPD took seats facing each other in his office at the Woodside Precinct. Arthur was in his fifties, had a rugged appearance, and his facial expression seemed to be announcing, "I've seen it all in the police business, and nothing can surprise me anymore."

"Ms. Bell, may I call you Amy?"

"Of course."

"OK, and I'm Art. Mark Traybert told me you'd probably be requesting to see me about the Filip Beron murder case. So I checked you out with some colleagues and also on the web. You are at the very top of your profession. So why did you decide to accept a case where Tony Capadora is a lead pipe cinch to be guilty as charged?"

"Well, Steven Atwood, who has known Tony since Tony was a child, hired me because he is absolutely certain that Tony could not possibly have committed this murder. I've dealt with Steven before, and he's no fool, so I accepted the case."

The detective smiled. "I'm sorry to tell you that this is as close as I've ever come in years to an open-and-shut case for conviction where the defendant denies all guilt. You are wasting your impressive talents on a killer who is virtually certain to spend the rest of his life in prison, unless Mark can pull a plea deal out of the DA's hat."

"Art, does this mean that the police are no longer investigating Filip's murder?"

"Correct, Amy, the case is all wrapped up. There are some very strong pieces of evidence, one of which is what amounts to a dying declaration, by the victim, writing down the name of his killer. Taken one at a time, each piece can be plausibly claimed to be not absolutely incriminating, but taken together, they form a virtually airtight case for conviction."

Amy nodded. "I agree that there's a strong case for conviction. But the burial of the murder weapon in Tony's backyard bothers me a great deal. The refilling was done in such a way as to make it totally obvious to the police that something had recently been buried in that place. That has all the makings of a frame-up. And the letters *CAPA* were leaked to the media on the Monday after the murder, so the killer knew that Tony was the person to frame."

Art shook his head. "You are giving Tony too much credit for intelligence in the area of pulling off a successful murder. He was an amateur. Amateurs make lots of mistakes. It looks like Tony tried to wipe the grip and trigger areas of the gun very carefully, to get rid of fingerprints. But being an amateur, he was very careless wiping the barrel. Luckily for him, the only two prints left there came from previous users.

"The serial number of the gun had been removed in a highly professional way. The gun was untraceable and obviously had been acquired illegally by Tony, probably recently, after he claimed Filip stole his song.

"Tony has no corroboration of his whereabouts during most of the period when the murder could have occurred. He was in the midst of an angry dispute with the victim. The murder weapon was found in his backyard. The victim's last action before dying was to write *CAPA* in his loose-leaf, with the final letter tailing off as if he expired at that point. Amy, you be a juror. What do you say?"

"I say Tony passed a polygraph test, administered by a top guy whom I retained, demonstrating that he had nothing to do with Filip's murder."

The detective laughed. "There are several defendants I've encountered who passed polygraphs, and then eventually, it was proven beyond any doubt that they were guilty. Polygraphs are not admissible in court for that very reason; they are totally unreliable."

"OK, put the polygraph aside. I say keep investigating. You may find someone who knew Filip and left one of the two prints found on the gun. That would supersede all the evidence against Tony and would exonerate him. You may find a different motive for someone to desire to kill Filip, which could lead to identifying serious suspects other than Tony."

Art smiled. "I can see why you're a great detective. You're never willing to quit; you pursue even the ten-million-to-one long shots. But here at the NYPD, where our time and resources are limited, we have to assign priorities. Ten-million-to-one long shots are at the bottom of our list of priorities."

Amy smiled and nodded. "I understand. If and when I hit on a ten-million-to-one long shot winner, I'll be back to see you. Before I leave, can you tell me if the killer stole anything from Filip or from Acme?"

The detective shook his head. "No, we don't have any reason to believe that anything at all was taken."

"Also, why would Tony bury the murder weapon in his own backyard, rather than bury it in the woods somewhere or throw it into a lake? That way, if the gun was found, it wouldn't immediately incriminate him."

"Tony may have wanted to be able to dig up the gun at a later date if he needed to use it again. That's why he didn't dump it elsewhere."

"Use it again?" Amy was not convinced by the detective's explanation.

"Sure, after all, Tony had already used it once." Amy moaned noticeably but let it go at that.

"Art, I may have some additional questions at some point, and if so, I hope I can contact you."

"Sure thing, Amy, it's been a pleasure meeting you." Art accompanied Amy out of the building.

Amy stopped at Subway for lunch and then returned to her Spy4U office. At one fifteen, she phoned her husband.

"Jerry, Detective Oteri says the case has been wrapped up. They aren't doing any more investigating. Art—that's the detective's first name—told me he feels that the totality of the evidence provides an airtight case for conviction. He said the reason that the gun was buried in a sloppy way, where the police could easily discover it, is because Tony was an amateur murderer and amateurs make mistakes."

"Did you tell Art about the polygraph?"

"I followed your advice"—Jeremy produced a big smile on his face—"and did not mention that Tony passed the polygraph regarding Filip stealing his song. I only said that the polygraph confirmed that he wasn't involved in the murder. Art completely pooh-poohed polygraphs. I didn't pursue the issue beyond that."

"Sweetheart, except for you and Steven, Tony seems to have no friends left in the world."

"Jerry, you're sure as hell right about that. But Art may be right about one thing. I may well be pursuing a ten-million-to-one long shot. I'd better be emotionally prepared to have my investigation produce absolutely nothing that can help Tony."

"You've had cases before, haven't you, where your investigations went nowhere?"

"Yes, but in this case, I know Tony is totally innocent of the murder, and also, I know his song was stolen from him. If I fail, Tony probably gets sent away for life, and much less importantly but still significant, he never receives recognition, nor financial compensation, for writing a hit song."

"Have you figured out the pretext you will use to convince your suspects to speak to you?"

"Yep. I'll tell them that there is now some significant evidence, which I can't discuss, showing that Tony is probably innocent. However, there is another suspect, whom video surveillance has shown following Filip on several occasions. I'll say I don't have his name yet, and I want to show them his photograph to see if they recognize him and if they ever saw him with or near Filip. I'll hand them a plastic sleeve containing a sheet of paper with this mystery man's photo on it. They'll presumably say they never saw him and return the sleeve to me. So hopefully, I'll then have their fingerprints on the sleeve."

Jeremy laughed. "Sweetheart, you are fiendishly clever! I never would have thought of that. Your strategy actually has a very good chance of working."

"Well, that kind of strategy has worked for me several times in the past. It makes it appear to the interviewees that they are not suspects. Also, it appeals to their curiosity and sounds believable.

"By the way, remember, this coming Saturday, we're having dinner and then bowling with the Mitchells. We're supposed to be there at five thirty, and we'll leave here a little after four thirty. So if you're playing tennis with Jason on Saturday, I want you home by three at the latest so you can get ready."

Her husband smiled. "Don't worry, I remembered our dinner date, so our tennis-court reservation on Saturday is from ten to noon."

"Good boy, Jerry, good boy! I think I'll reward you when I get home for being such a good boy!" Amy immediately hung up.

Saturday, August 13, 2016

Amy and Jeremy arrived at the Mitchells' apartment at 5:25 p.m., and the foursome spent about a half hour observing, playing with, and discussing Aurora. Then Cathy's mother arrived to babysit. At that point, Cathy made an announcement.

"I have some bad news and also some good news. The bad news is that Eddie twisted his ankle yesterday. It's feeling a lot better today, but he can't go bowling this evening.

"The good news is that I have switched our six-thirty dinner reservation to Reilly's Pub. It's only a few blocks from here, and at seven forty-five on Saturday evenings, they run a trivia contest, with prizes of thirty, twenty, and ten dollars for the first-, second-, and third-place teams."

Amy smiled broadly. "Of course, I hope Eddie is entirely better real soon, but I love trivia contests!"

Jeremy wasn't as sanguine. "I like trivia too, but I remember what's happened with you during trivia contests on cruises, particularly with our Caribbean cruise on the Superior Titan. You lost your cool, arguing with the quizmaster over what were the correct answers."

"Yes, Jerry, but those trivia answers on the cruise were all screwed up. In a place like Reilly's, with weekly trivia, I'm sure they do a professional job. Don't worry about me; I'll just be having fun."

Eddie was relieved. "I'm glad my injury won't stop us from enjoying a fun evening activity. So I guess we should get out of here."

Everyone thanked Cathy's mother for enabling them to go out together for the evening, and after a leisurely walk, they arrived at Reilly's three minutes early. Their table was ready, and while sipping wine after ordering their main courses, Cathy had a question.

"Amy, Eddie tells me you may need to try to match up various suspects' fingerprints with prints you already have. What kind of case are you investigating?"

Amy related some of the details of the *Filip Beron* case. "So if a print from one of my suspects matches a print on the gun, it would be pretty conclusive evidence that my guy is innocent and the suspect is guilty."

Amy's best girlfriend was impressed. "Sounds like an interesting case. What if none of the suspects' prints match the prints on the gun?"

"Then my guy may well be totally screwed and is likely to end up in prison for life, even though he's innocent."

"Amy," inquired Eddie, "have you interviewed any of your suspects yet?"

"No, not yet."

"Well, be sure to tell me what happens."

They all enjoyed steak dinners and had chocolate cake for dessert. At seven forty-five, Sean, the quizmaster, introduced the game.

"Hello, players, the trivia will start shortly. Teams can have from one to six members. Put away all phones, and put them on vibrate. Don't say answers loudly enough to allow other teams to hear you. There will be forty questions, shown on the screen behind me, which I will also read out loud. You have two minutes to submit the answer to each question, by entering the answer on your tablet. Whatever is on your tablet at the end of the two minutes is your answer. Then I will announce the correct answer and go on to the next question.

"All answers have been double-checked for accuracy. And the decision of the quizmaster—that's me—is final. Each prize is for the team as a whole, not one prize per player. Each team has to choose a captain, who will enter the answers on the tablet and be in charge of any cash prize the team receives.

"This will be general trivia, with questions on sports, politics, history, geography, literature, current events, and show business. There are fourteen teams who have registered. In case of a tie for first at the end of the game, there will be a tiebreaking question. We will begin with question one in two minutes."

"I'll be captain," announced Amy as she reached over and grabbed the tablet. This came as no surprise whatsoever to the other three, and they smiled at each other.

Question 1 was an easy question on the Oscars. Amy immediately typed in the answer and showed it to her teammates, who all nodded in agreement. Their answer was correct, and Amy assumed that the vast majority of teams also got it right.

Question 2 was, "What is the longest river that is always in New York State?" Amy said, "I know it for sure," and then typed in "Mohawk" on the tablet and showed it around. Cathy and Eddie scratched their heads. Jeremy said, "Are you certain?" and Amy responded, "Absolutely, and I'll bet most of the other teams put down the wrong answer."

After two minutes, Sean announced the correct answer, which was the Hudson. Amy immediately stood up. "Sean, the Hudson River is only a few miles from where we are now. When it passes Manhattan and the Bronx, it is half in New York and half in New Jersey. So it is not always in New York."

Sean gave Amy a not-so-friendly look and spoke in a tone Amy felt was condescending. "If a river is entirely in New York in some places and half in New York in other places, then it is never entirely out of New York, so it is always in New York."

"That's ridiculous," replied Amy, who was still standing and was now glaring at the quizmaster. "If you are driving on the George Washington Bridge or Lincoln Tunnel, you pass a sign in the middle, saying 'New Jersey.' If a river is sometimes in New Jersey, it can't be always in New York."

People at other tables were getting restless. Some shouted out, "Sit down!" Sean didn't respond directly to Amy's argument. Instead, he said, "The decision of the quizmaster is final. On to question 3." Amy sat down as her teammates exhibited smiles of embarrassment.

Things proceeded without incident for quite a while. Question 18 was a particularly difficult one: "In the only baseball World Series perfect game ever, whom did Don Larsen strike out to end the game?" Amy looked around at the nearby tables, and everyone had blank looks on their faces. But Eddie had a big smile on his face. He whispered, "I know that because he has the same last name as me. It's Dale Mitchell." Eddie was indeed correct. Amy suspected that her team was the only one that got it right.

Question 26 was a tough question regarding the TV series *Seinfeld*. Cathy, a big *Seinfeld* fan, knew the answer.

Amy was optimistic that her team was in the running to win. There were several questions where her team had been clueless, but she felt that almost all the other teams were probably stumped too.

The smooth sailing ended with question 33, which was, "What is the largest lake, in surface area, in the world?"

Cathy whispered, "Lake Superior," and looked at her teammates. Eddie shrugged his shoulders, and Jeremy whispered, "I agree." But Amy shook her head vigorously. "The Caspian Sea is by far the biggest lake," she whispered. "The word 'sea' is a misnomer. It is definitely a lake and not a sea."

The rest of the team grudgingly accepted Amy's assurances and went with her answer. Then Sean announced that the correct answer is Lake Superior. Amy again rose. "Excuse me."

There was an immediate reaction from other tables, with such comments as "It's her again" and "Sit down and shut up." But Amy went on.

"The Caspian Sea is the world's largest lake. It is much larger than Lake Superior."

Someone from another team yelled out, "The Caspian Sea is a sea, jerk!" This resulted in a round of laughter in the pub. But Amy was not amused. "A sea is an ocean or is directly connected to an ocean. A lake is inland. The Caspian Sea is misnamed. It is inland and is a lake."

Sean again displayed his unfriendly look and condescending tone, at least in Amy's opinion. "We try to make the questions easy to understand for the average person. If the name of a body of water has the word 'lake' in it, then it's a lake. If it has 'sea' in it, then it's a sea. The decision of the quizmaster is final. The answer is 'Lake Superior.' Ma'am, you can sit down now, we're going on to question 34." Most of the pub erupted in applause.

The fortieth and final question was, "Who ran for VP as Barry Goldwater's running mate in 1964?" Amy whispered, "I'm embarrassed. I was a political science major, and I don't know."

But Jeremy saved the day. "It's William Miller. And why aren't there any trivia questions on probability or insurance?" The table broke into laughter at this question by Amy's actuary husband.

Amy was still very optimistic as Sean totaled up the scores. Then he announced the results. "Teams 4, 7, and 13 are in a three-way tie for first with a score of 33 out of 40. Team 9 is fourth with 32 points, and team 2 is fifth with 31. So the three teams tied for first will now answer this tiebreaker: 'In what year was the Boston Massacre?' The team whose answer is closest to the correct year wins."

Amy's team was team 9, in fourth place. Now she was in a rage, but she kept her voice down. "The year of the Boston Massacre was 1770. But we should have 34 points, so we should have been the outright winners."

Cathy was not convinced. "Amy, what if one or more of the top three teams had 'Mohawk River' and also 'Caspian Sea' as their answers? Then they would still be ahead of us, regardless. Even if they had only one of them correct, they'd be tied with us for first."

"You have a point. But 'Mohawk' and 'Caspian' were tough questions, and no other team joined in my protests, so your scenario is not too likely. And I have the correct answer to the tiebreaker. Let's see if they do."

"Amy," pleaded her best girlfriend, "whatever happens, don't ask the other teams whether they had 'Mohawk' or 'Caspian.' And don't go up and continue your dispute with Sean."

Amy nodded. "You have my word, I'll hold my tongue."

At this point, Sean announced, "The correct answer is 1770. The submitted answers are 1772, 1773, and 1775. So team 7 is the winner, and team 13 is second, with team 4 in third. Congratulations to our top three teams, and thanks to everyone for participating."

It was all Amy could do to contain herself. "So we would have won the tiebreaker. Therefore, we would have won the trivia unless one of the top three teams had both 'Mohawk' and 'Caspian' as their answers."

Jeremy had been punching in things on his iPhone since the three-way tie was announced. "Sweetheart, I looked on the Internet, and your answers of 'Mohawk' and 'Caspian' were indeed correct. For the right answer to be 'Lake Superior,' rather than 'Caspian Sea,' the question should have asked for the largest *freshwater* lake in the world, as opposed to just the largest lake. So when they double-checked their answers, they probably missed the significance of the word 'freshwater' and, therefore, left that word out of the trivia question."

Amy was still quite agitated. "Jerry, if you could verify my answer using your iPhone, then why the hell couldn't Sean have used his iPhone to verify my answers after I objected to his answers?"

Her husband shook his head. "I don't think they generally do that in trivia games, because it's not feasible. It takes up a lot of extra time and opens it up for people to find various different answers on the web and have no way of determining which is actually correct. But at least we all now know that we probably actually won the trivia."

As Jeremy was speaking, a kind-looking man, walking slowly with a cane, who appeared to be around eighty years old, approached their table and smiled at Amy. "Young lady, you were right in your two protests, but you have to lighten up and not get yourself so excited and upset. They make mistakes like that quite often in this kind of trivia game. The prize money isn't large enough to spoil your fun when they announce the wrong answer, and you had the right one. Trust my advice; I've been playing trivia at places like this for many years."

Amy responded appreciatively. "Thanks for coming over and taking the time to speak to me. Was your team in the top three?"

He shook his head. "No, we had 28 right. But we did have 'Caspian Sea,' so we really had 29." He smiled at Amy and exited the pub.

"He's a sweet man," said Amy, "but he was wrong about one thing. With me, it's not in any way about the money. It's about the principle. My response would have been exactly the same if there were no prizes at all. However, he's right about the rest of what he said. This is just supposed to be fun. I hope I didn't spoil the fun for you guys."

"No worries, Amy," said Eddie. "The whole thing was actually rather amusing to me"—Cathy and Jeremy smiled and nodded in agreement—"but I think you should just accept the fact that screw-ups with regard to the answers are part of the game and not worth getting upset over. And I'm officially declaring victory for our team!"

"Yeah," said Jeremy, "to celebrate our win, let's schedule one of those two-hour boat trips, leaving from Manhattan, which go up and down the Hudson River. And most importantly, I think they always stay on the New York State side of the river!" Nods and laughter from everyone at the table.

When they arrived home, Amy showed her husband a black-and-white photograph of a man who appeared to be in his thirties or forties walking on a city sidewalk. "Jerry, do you recognize this man?"

Jeremy stared at the man for a few seconds. "It's not a great photo; his face is not crystal clear. I can't identify him, but I think I've seen him before somewhere, although I have no idea where or when. It actually looks like it might be a surveillance photo."

Amy smiled. "You know, that might make a good line for a song. 'Who knows where or when?' If Filip weren't dead, I would submit it to him, to use in a song." Jeremy got his wife's joke and laughed.

"But in fact, you've never seen him, anywhere. He's been dead for fifty years. He lived in Toronto and was the grandfather of a colleague of mine at Spy4U. I'm going to show it to my suspects and tell them that it is a surveillance photo of my new suspect in Filip's murder."

Jeremy laughed again. "Maybe all your suspects will also think they've seen him before. He's got that kind of face. Who do you want to interview first?"

"Maybe Karen Maddox. Morton told me that Filip stole Karen from Bart Mallon, his colleague at Acme. They split up a few months later, but Karen and Bart never got back together."

"What kind of motive would Karen have had to kill Filip?"

"I have no idea whatsoever, but I have to start somewhere."

Tuesday, August 16, 2016

Amy walked to Times Square Station and took the N train to Lexington Avenue. She transferred to the Number 6 train and got off at Seventy-Seventh Street. From there, it was only a four-minute walk to Karen Maddox's high-rise apartment building. At 11:15 a.m., she identified herself to the doorman, who phoned Karen to receive her approval to let Amy into the building. Having accomplished that, he opened the door and motioned Amy in the direction of the elevators.

Eventually, Karen ushered her guest into a well-furnished one-bedroom apartment on the eleventh floor. Karen was blond, very tall—but not as tall as Filip, who was six foot one—thin, and very attractive. Amy accepted Karen's offer of a Diet Pepsi. "Amy, I was very intrigued by your e-mail. You think Tony Capadora may be innocent and you have a new suspect? By the way, did Tony hire you?"

"A decades-long friend of Tony hired me to try to help Tony. I have uncovered some significant evidence, which, unfortunately, I can't discuss at this point, indicating that Tony is probably innocent. I want to show you a photo of my new suspect. It's from a surveillance camera, and it's not a great photo, but I think his face is pretty clear." Amy handed Karen the plastic sleeve with the photo in it, and her hostess studied it.

"This man had apparently been following close behind Filip, tailing him, on several occasions in the weeks before Filip was murdered. I don't know his name. Do you recognize him? Or have you seen him before, maybe with Filip or hanging out in his proximity?"

"You know, I think I have seen this guy. Maybe at Louie's Lounge in the Crawford Hotel, where I sing, two shows an evening, five evenings a week."

"At what times do you do your shows? Maybe my husband, Jerry, and I can come see you perform."

"I do a seventy-five-minute show at seven thirty and also at ten thirty, every evening except for Sunday and Monday. Louie's Lounge also serves great dinners."

"So maybe you'll see us there. Did you ever see the man in this photo with Filip or following him?"

"No, if I saw him, it was at the Crawford Hotel."

Amy smiled and nodded. "OK, thanks, I need the photo back." Karen returned the sleeve, and Amy put it back into her folder. "I'll e-mail you a copy of the photo so you can look at it again; maybe you'll remember something additional.

"Now, to give me the best chance to solve the case, I need to know as much as possible about Filip. So can you tell me about your time with him?"

"Well, it wasn't a first-rate experience, to say the least. Bart thinks Filip stole me away from him, but that's not true. It had reached the point where I knew it was over with us, even if Bart hadn't yet figured that out. I made the first move with Filip, and he immediately took me up on it.

"After a couple of secret dates with Filip, I told Bart we were through. Then Filip and I became open about our relationship. But Bart continues, to this day, to think that Filip took me away from him."

Amy interrupted, "Have you told Bart that it's not true?"

"Yes, once, while I was still seeing Filip. He said he didn't believe me, and I never mentioned it again. In fact, I have hardly spoken with Bart since then.

"Anyhow, things eventually went downhill with Filip. Before I officially broke up with Bart, and for a few weeks after, Filip was a perfect gentleman in every way. But after that, he started to become bullying and impatient with me. The next stage was shouting at me and calling me names. Finally, when I spoke to him and called him out on this behavior, he hit me, on two occasions. Now I know you'll say that I should have dumped him after the first time he hit me."

Amy nodded. "Actually, I'd say you should have dumped Filip after the shouting and name-calling, assuming it happened several times."

"It did, but I was an infatuated fool, and I gave Filip too many second chances."

"Karen, is there anything else about Filip I should know that might conceivably help me find out the identity of this man in the photo?"

Her hostess was silent for about ten seconds, then she spoke. "Well, I am not one hundred percent positive, but I believe Filip was taking drugs—I mean illegal drugs."

"What makes you believe that?"

"I'm not knowledgeable about the specific effects of various drugs, but there were occasions when Filip seemed 'out of it,' and he had that dazed look in his eyes. It's hard for me to be more specific.

"Also, I once overheard Filip talking on the phone with some-one about arranging a meeting to buy some 'stuff'—I think that's the word he used. Based on some of the things he said, I'm pretty sure he was talking to someone who also worked for Acme. When he realized I could hear what he was saying, Filip immediately hung up and gave me some ridiculous story about him possibly buying some gold coins as an investment and also in case of an emergency situation where it would be useful to have them."

"Karen, what was the time period during which you were with Filip?"

"During mid-March through late May of this year."

Amy thanked Karen for her assistance and then exited the apartment.

After lunch at Panera, when she got back to Spy4U, Amy phoned Morton. After the pleasantries, Amy had a request. "Can you provide me with a list of people who work for Acme, whose work location is the Acme headquarters all or most of the time? Also, can you get me their contact information?"

"Sure, there are about fifteen of them. I'll e-mail you a list by tomorrow. So you still think there's a chance Tony is not the killer?"

"Yes, I do. And thanks so much for all your help."

Next, she phoned Detective Oteri. "Hi, Art, this is Amy Bell. I have a question for you. Did you find anything unusual or interesting on Filip's phone or computer?"

"We did check both carefully. Nothing unusual on either."

"What numbers did Filip call most frequently on his phone?"

"All the people he frequently called were colleagues of Filip at Acme Melodies. Three, in particular, were called very frequently."

"Can you give me the names of those three people he called most frequently?"

"Sure, give me a couple of hours. I'll e-mail you the top three." Amy thanked the detective for his assistance and hung up.

Amy got home at ten past five. She and Jeremy enjoyed Chinese takeout for dinner, then Amy updated her husband on the day's developments.

"Karen provided a lot of useful information. First of all, she confirmed that Filip hit her twice, which was a cause of her breaking up with him, along with his behavior toward her generally becoming nastier. She said she actually came on to Filip, rather than vice versa, when she knew she was going to end her relationship with Bart. But Bart still thinks Filip stole her from him.

"Now for the juicy stuff. Karen is pretty sure that Filip was taking some sort of illegal drugs, and she thinks someone at Acme was selling the drugs to Filip. Morton has agreed to e-mail me a list of all the Acme people. I'll ask Eddie to find out if any of them has some kind of past record involving drugs.

"And talking about Acme people, I requested and received from Detective Oteri the names of the three people Filip phoned most frequently. They all work for Acme. In order, they are Barry Garner, Dennis Bartow, and Kevin Franco. We know why he phoned Barry so often; he was Filip's talent liaison and friend. So I'll bet that either Dennis or Kevin was selling him drugs."

Jeremy nodded. "That drug angle could be very significant. Lots of people have been killed over drugs. Did you get Karen's fingerprints?"

"I sure hope so. I'll give the sleeve, as well as a copy of the two prints from the gun, to Brad Zelman, Spy4U's fingerprint guy. He'll see if there's a match. But I'm almost certain that Karen had nothing to do with the murder.

"By the way, Karen said the man in the photo looked familiar; he may have been in attendance at one of her five-days-a-week singing performances at the Crawford Hotel. I told her we might come to one of her shows. We can also have dinner there prior to the show. Are you interested?"

"Sure, why not? Dinner and Karen's show; sounds like a fun night out."

Wednesday, August 17, 2016

At 10:15 a.m., Amy, at her Spy4U office, received an e-mail from Morton containing the names and contact information for the fifteen Acme people. She immediately forwarded the list to Eddie and then phoned him.

"Eddie, I need a little more assistance."

"Amy, I knew all along that your first request wouldn't be the end of it. So what additional 'little thing' would you like me to do for you?"

"I just forwarded to you an e-mail containing a list of fifteen Acme employees. I need to know which of them, if any, have police records, particularly involving illegal drugs."

"Only fifteen?" Amy laughed. "OK, Amy, I'll see what I can do."

"Thanks so much, Eddie."

After lunch, Amy took the subway to Queens, to Rego Park, where she rang the bell in the lobby of an apartment building on Saunders Street and was buzzed in by Sally Jarvis, the second of Filip's three former girlfriends. Sally's two-bedroom apartment was on the fourth floor. Sally was tall, thin, and blond—Amy thought she might have detected a pattern—and quite talkative, without any prompting.

"Amy, please pardon the clutter. My roommate Barbara and I both have the fault of being messy. She's at work. Today's one of my days off; I'm a server at the Cavandish Steak House." Amy recognized the name of one of the city's best and most expensive restaurants.

Amy accepted Sally's offer of a Diet Coke, and her hostess continued. "So you have a photo to show me? It was quite a shock to find out that Filip had been murdered, but he had turned out to be quite a scumbag—pardon my French—so that kind of lessened my horror."

"Yes, I want you to look at the man's photo. I don't know his name, but several surveillance camera photos have shown him walking a few feet behind Filip." Amy gave Sally the sleeve with the photo. She studied it for about twenty seconds while putting her hand to her forehead and biting her lip.

"No, I don't remember ever seeing this man before. Of course, I can't be sure." She handed the sleeve back to Amy.

"Well, thanks for looking at it. Can you tell me about your time with Filip?"

"Sure. We literally bumped into each other at a supermarket; it was in April of last year. He was tall and very good-looking. He had an exotic Eastern European accent. He immediately told me he had a hit song, 'I'll Never Believe It.' He asked if I'd heard it. When I told him no, he invited me to his apartment to watch his music video.

"For some reason, I threw caution to the wind and took him up on his offer. The song was very catchy, and Filip was a perfect gentleman. We started dating, and before too long, he stopped being a gentleman. He became dominating and verbally abusive. Then he became physically abusive. When he hit me, I ended it. The whole relationship lasted about seven weeks."

"Is there anything else you can tell me about Filip that might help me identify his killer?"

"Not really. And you're saying the guy they arrested didn't do it?"

"Yes, the evidence I've uncovered definitely points away from him."

"Well, good luck finding the real killer; I'm sorry I couldn't have been more helpful."

"Oh no, Sally, you've been very helpful; I truly appreciate you taking the time to talk to me."

Amy got back to Spy4U at three thirty and found a message to call Chester. She did, and he asked her to come over to his office. When she arrived, Chester had a question. "Amy, how are things going with the *Tony Capadora* case?"

"I'm starting to collect fingerprints from my suspects to see if they might match one of the two prints on the murder weapon.

There are also a few other possible leads, but no real progress yet."

"Remember, Amy, this sounds like a very tough case, and as I've said before, all you can do is your best. It's not possible to pull off a miracle every time."

Amy smiled. "Yeah, if I get a fingerprint match, it would indeed be a miracle. But I assume that's not why I'm here, in your office."

"You're right. Do you recognize the name Blake Donnell?"

"No, should I?"

"Actually, he's a very wealthy and well-connected patron of the arts. I've known him socially for many years. I just received a phone call from Blake. He wants to hire you regarding a matter that he says appears to be very minor but is very important to him. And he's willing to pay big bucks. He specifically asked for you."

"Do you know where he got my name?"

"I asked him. Blake said one of his close friends recommended you but asked that their name not be revealed. This matter has something to with his only child, a son, Paul, who is nineteen years old. Blake doesn't think Paul is the brightest star in the sky, intellectually. He used his connections to get Paul into Stenman College, a small private commuter college on the Upper East Side. I'll bet you've never heard of Stenman; I certainly hadn't."

"You're right," interrupted Amy.

"Anyhow, can you meet with Blake here in my office tomorrow morning at ten? As usual, it'll be your call as to whether to accept the case."

Amy nodded. "Sure, I can meet with Blake, and if I think there's a chance I can help, I'll do it. But I can't spare more than three days, at most."

"Fine, and Amy, I fully understand your time constraints." After another minute or two of small talk, she exited Chester's office.

When Amy arrived home at five, she was greeted by her husband, wearing only his underpants and a T-shirt. He had just showered after arriving back home from an afternoon tennis match.

Amy was very envious of Jeremy's working schedule. As a freelance actuarial consultant, he did have to attend various meetings with clients at their offices, but in general, he worked out of his apartment. He made his own hours, so if there was an opportunity, like today, for afternoon tennis, he was usually free to grab it. But of course, Jeremy was a math and probability genius and making very good money. And also, she could ask Jeremy to do grocery shopping for her and bring food home for dinner, which was no small benefit.

Amy looked at her husband's scantily clad body, showed him a coy, sexy smile, and made an announcement. "Jerry, I want to update you on the day's developments, and I want to hear your feedback. But you usually give your most thoughtful feedback when you are totally naked. So, off with your underwear, now!"

Jeremy could think of no suitable response to this order other than to do what he was told. So he took off the two things he had on and stood there nude.

"Good boy! Why don't we sit in the living room?" They proceeded to that room, and Amy presented her update. "So, Jerry, what are your nude impressions? And this is one hell of enjoyable way for me to hear what you have to say!"

"Well, it's now pretty obvious that Filip had a problem with violence; he probably struck all his girlfriends."

Amy nodded. "Agreed."

"And switching topics, I think it's rather distasteful to tell a social acquaintance—either before or after you employ his firm to do an investigation—that your son is not very smart."

"You know, Jerry, you're right; I hadn't considered that. It was a low-class thing for Blake to tell that to Mr. Murray about his son. It would be different if that information is critical to solving the case, but I strongly doubt it. Of course, I haven't found out yet what the case may entail. I'll find out tomorrow morning at ten."

Jeremy changed the subject again. "Sweetheart, I assume that if Eddie discovers that one of the fifteen Acme people—especially if it's Dennis or Kevin—has some sort of police record involving drugs, then you'll be pretty confident that this person was Filip's drug pusher, and that person would become a major suspect in Filip's murder."

Amy nodded. "For sure. But even if it's not one of those two, if another Acme employee has such a police record, that person becomes a major suspect. And yes, you make such thoughtful observations when you are totally naked. Why don't you get dressed now for dinner?"

Jeremy was trying to think of a suitable reply, but he drew a blank. So he just proceeded to the bedroom to put on some clothes.

Thursday, August 18, 2016

At 10:00 a.m., when Amy entered Chester's office, Blake and Paul Donnell were already there. Chester introduced them to her; they shook hands and took seats.

Amy knew that Blake was fifty years old. He was five foot ten, very smartly dressed and looked ten years younger. Amy decided that Blake was wearing a hairpiece. Paul was thin and a little taller than his father. Amy got the impression that Paul was very uncomfortable, almost scared. As Blake began to speak, Paul's eyes were directed at the rug, and that was where they mainly stayed.

"Amy, Chester has informed me that you have a very full schedule, and should you decide to take it on, you can only afford to spend, at most, three days on my case. I'm willing to accept that. If you can't make progress after three days, I'll understand if you stop at that point.

"First, let me explain that I am a big fan of live theatre, and I'm lucky to have the financial resources to be an 'angel' for various off Broadway shows. I provide financial support, as well as some guidance, based on my experience. However, I do not publicize my involvement in the plays that I back. I prefer to stay in the background.

"Currently, I'm backing *Very Valuable*, a new play which opened last month at the Stanley Theatre in Greenwich Village. The plot concerns a grandson who always disparaged the advice about life given to him by his grandfather, but after the grandfather died, he slowly began to realize that the advice he had been given was right on target. In other words, the advice turned out to be very valuable, hence the title of the play."

Blake reached into the inside pocket of his sports jacket and pulled out two tickets. He handed them to Amy. "Here are two free passes to see the play. They're good for any performance. You'll sit in two of the six seats reserved solely for my use.

"Anyhow, this past Friday evening, Paul and four of his Stenman College men friends attended a college awards ceremony. Actually, it's a big stretch to call them 'friends.' I've met them, and they're basically dumb, spoiled, unreliable losers. Afterwards, they went to Ralph's parents' apartment for drinks and desserts. Ralph is one of the four friends, and all four, as well as Paul, still live at home." At this point, Paul's head was facing straight down. Amy felt very sorry for him.

"Before Paul left for the ceremony, I gave him two passes, the same as yours, for *Very Valuable*. I told him to take the girl he was dating to see the show on the following weekend. Paul put the passes in his sports jacket, in the inside pocket—jackets were required for the awards ceremony. Paul was in the habit of putting things in his jacket pocket. He told me that in addition to the theatre tickets, he had put five Powerball lottery tickets there that evening, as well as six fifty-dollar bills, in case of emergency. Isn't that right, Paul?"

Paul didn't look up. "Yes, Father, that's right."

"Paul," Amy interrupted, "do you carry a wallet?"

"Yes he does," Blake responded, looking at Amy and without glancing at his son. "In his pants pocket. But he says he wants it to be very thin so the pocket doesn't bulge. Also, putting emergency money in his jacket does add an extra level of prudence."

Amy nodded. "That makes some sense."

Blake continued. "When Paul and his friends arrived at Ralph's parents' apartment after the ceremony, they all took off their jackets and left them on a sofa in the den. The apartment is large and swanky. Ralph's parents were there, as well as their longtime housekeeper, whom they had hired to serve desserts and drinks at the event.

"At around eleven, Paul's three friends, other than Ralph, left together. They lived near each other and had called for a car to take the three of them home. Paul lived only a few blocks away from Ralph, so when he left, a couple of minutes later, he was able to walk home. After Paul arrived home, he discovered that his inside jacket pocket was empty. Someone had obviously entered the den at Ralph's apartment and removed the contents of the inside pocket."

"I assume," Amy remarked, "that Paul has checked all the other pockets in the jacket."

"Oh yes, and they were empty."

Paul looked up, and Amy could see a hopeless look on his face. "Father, do we have to do this? The stuff that was taken isn't worth doing this to me, not to mention my friends."

"Son, it's not the value of what was taken. It's a question of someone being a thief. And it's almost certainly one of your four friends. If Amy can identify the thief, I'm not saying we should take any public action against him. I'm not even saying you have to tell him you know. But it is important that you do know. In life, you have to know whom you can and cannot trust. So I'm not doing this *to* you. I'm doing this *for* you."

Amy nodded. "Paul, your father has a point. Here's what I suggest. Tell your four friends that your father has retained me to see if any of them saw anything at the apartment that may help me determine what happened. Tell them I said that sometimes, when interviewed by a good detective, people mention something they didn't realize had any importance but may be critical in solving a case. Tell them you really need their help. I can meet them, individually, one at a time, at the college, or at any other convenient location. I can do the interviews tomorrow, if that can be arranged. Are classes running now at Stenman?"

Amy was looking at Paul when she asked this question, but it was Blake who nodded and replied. "Yes, they run two consecutive six-week summer sessions. The second one ends next week. Paul and his four friends are taking classes during the current session."

"Paul," inquired Amy, "exactly what have you told your friends regarding what was taken from your jacket pocket?"

"All I've said is that some money and a few other things were taken."

"You didn't specifically mention the amount of money or the lottery and show tickets?"

"No, I didn't specifically mention any of that."

"Before your father gave you the two theatre tickets last Friday, were you aware of the name or plot of *Very Valuable*, the new play he was backing?"

"No, I am aware that he backs various plays, but I had no knowledge at all about this particular one."

"Blake, I want you and Paul to understand that I'm accepting the case, but while I may be a good detective, I am not a magician or a clairvoyant. There is a very substantial likelihood that I will not be able to identify the thief."

"Understood," replied Blake.

Paul looked a bit relieved. "So I should tell them that they may be witnesses, not that they are suspects, right?"

Amy smiled. "That's exactly right. Tell them I need their help to draw out something they may have seen or heard. And be sure not to give them any additional information about what was taken from your jacket pocket."

Paul smiled—for the first time during the meeting—at his father and said, "OK, maybe this will be all right. I'll do it."

Blake appeared very pleased. "Great! So, Amy, you'll give it the old college try—no double entendre intended."

"Blake, may I ask who recommended me to you?"

"I promised the person who recommended you that I would not reveal their name. But that person told me that you are a genius at getting people to incriminate themselves when you interview them."

Amy turned red. "Well, I always carefully plan out what I'm going to ask my interviewees. And I do listen very closely to what they say. By the way, is it OK if my husband, Jeremy, joins me during the interviews? He often helps me out with my tough cases."

Blake looked at Paul, who nodded. "No problem. Is he as smart as you?"

"In probability, he's much smarter; Jerry's an actuary. In detective work, he's not as smart, but he's very logical, as well as extremely sexy and good-looking." The whole room burst out laughing. Then Amy shook hands with the two visitors and exited Chester's office.

At eleven thirty, she phoned her husband and related what was said at the meeting. "So I assume you can accompany me to the interviews."

"Sure, sweetheart, I don't have any other time-specific obligations for the next week, other than weekend tennis."

"I'm hoping I can complete them all tomorrow, at Stenman College. It's on East Eighty-Third Street. Have you ever heard of Stenman?"

"No."

"Neither have I. I got the impression from Blake that it's a cake-walk school for mediocre students whose wealthy parents can afford their outrageous tuition."

Jeremy laughed. "Wouldn't employers be aware of that? Is a degree from Stenman of any serious value?"

"Sadly, yes. A college degree is, in many ways, a 'union card' that is absolutely essential nowadays, in many job fields, to allow the possibility of employment. In other jobs, you can't be promoted without it. It doesn't matter if you learned anything at college, it's the degree that matters. This is totally unfair and, in many ways, counterproductive, but that's the way it is.

"Jerry, you studied actuarial science at Northeastern, so you were learning the exact skills you needed for your future career. But that's not the case for most liberal-arts students at any college. I majored in political science at CCNY, which is a first-rate school. As you know, I had planned to become a lawyer until working at Spy4U changed my direction. I enjoyed my classes, but how much useful stuff did I actually learn?"

Her husband smiled broadly. "Sweetheart, you learned enough to be a star at trivia!" They both laughed heartily. "Also, from what you're telling me, Blake treats his son in a very conde-scending way, making the young man very uncomfortable."

"Jerry, that's an understatement. I feel very sorry for Paul. I understand that Blake is a widower, so Paul doesn't have a sec-ond parent to treat him more warmly and respectfully."

"Do you plan to speak to Blake about this at some point?"

"Yes, if I can find an appropriate time and place to do so. Why don't you meet me at Big Tony's for dinner at five thirty?"

"Will do."

Amy left Spy4U at five o'clock and took a twenty-five-minute leisurely walk to Big Tony's, on the East Side, which was one of her favorite restaurants in Manhattan. As usual, Big Tony was there at the entrance to greet diners, many of whom marveled at how Tony's immense girth seemed even more massive than it was the last time they came there. She observed Jeremy waiting for her on a sofa in the lobby. He rose and kissed her, then they were led to a table.

After giving the waiter their dinner orders, and while sipping wine, Amy provided her husband with some news. "Jerry, the four interviews are all set up for tomorrow. Apparently, from noon to two on Friday afternoons are the 'club hours' at Stenman College. No classes meet at that time. So that's when I'll meet with the four friends, in an empty classroom. Here's the schedule: Ralph Macklin at twelve twenty, Michael Pell at twelve forty, Danny Orland at one, and finally, Carmine Toro at one twenty.

"Why don't you meet me at Spy4U at quarter to eleven tomorrow morning? We can have an early lunch together then head for Stenman. As usual, at the interviews, I want you to sit with me, smile, and observe. If you come up with a question I should ask, whisper it in my ear. After each interview, I'll want to hear your impressions. But I won't tell you if I suspect anyone in particular until all four interviews have finished."

Jeremy smiled and nodded. "Sweetheart, I know the drill. Do you have some sort of plan for what you'll ask them at the interviews?"

Now Amy nodded. "I have several ideas. But sadly, I think the most likely result of the four interviews is that I will make no progress at all. I may not even have any kind of direction for further investigation. And remember, in any case, I can't spend more than three days on this. But as they say, nothing ventured, nothing gained."

Friday, August 19, 2016

At 10:45 a.m., Jeremy arrived at the Spy4U offices, located in the Forties near Ninth Avenue. In the lobby, he smiled and waved at the receptionist, who recognized Jeremy and buzzed him in. He arrived at Amy's office, said hello to the secretary, knocked three times on Amy's door, paused, and then knocked twice more. Amy recognized the pattern, opened the door, and gave her husband a big kiss.

Five minutes later, they exited the building and proceeded to Subway, where they shared a foot-long meatball sandwich and ate chocolate-chip cookies for dessert. Then they took the subway to Eighty-Sixth Street and Lexington Avenue. After a ten-minute walk, they reached their destination address.

Jeremy was confused. "This is a college? It looks like a nine-story apartment building."

Amy pointed to a sign over the entrance. "Look, it says 'Stenman College.' So we're at the right place."

They entered the building and, once in the lobby, were immediately greeted by Paul Donnell, who, Amy thankfully observed, was not accompanied by his father. Paul shook hands with both visitors.

"Hello, Amy, and also hello, Jeremy, I presume."

Amy's husband nodded. "Yes, I'm Jeremy."

"Welcome to Stenman College. I'll check you in at the front desk as my guests, and I'll get your day passes. Then we'll go to the classroom where you can interview my four friends. The schedule which you already have is still in effect. So you'll see Ralph first, at twelve twenty, then Michael, Danny, and finally, Carmine. Is all that OK with you guys?"

"Sure," replied Amy.

Paul led Amy and Jeremy to a classroom on the fourth floor, whereupon he exited the room. Jeremy was impressed. "Everything in this room is so modern. The desk and chairs look brand-new"—he sat down—"and these seats are cushioned and comfortable. There's a screen which can be pulled down over the blackboard and a projector in the back. There are several TVs all around the room."

Amy smiled. "That's what outrageously high tuition can do for a college. It wasn't at all like this at CCNY."

At twelve twenty, Ralph Macklin arrived for his interview. He was five foot eleven, fit, and trim. He was dressed smartly. Amy decided he looked like a preppy, as she understood the term. The three exchanged introductions and took seats. Ralph spoke first and had a smile on his face.

"Amy, I am acquainted with Paul's father, and knowing him, I completely understand why he retained your services."

Amy laughed. "Ralph, I get your meaning. But let me go over the events of a week ago, as I understand them. You and your four Stenman College classmates and friends came back to your apartment after an evening awards ceremony at the college. You all put your jackets on a sofa in the den—"

"All except for me," interrupted Ralph. "I put my jacket in my bedroom closet."

"I stand corrected. Other than the five of you, the only other people present in the apartment were your parents and your housekeeper, who served drinks and desserts. At around eleven, Michael, Danny, and Carmine left together and took a car to their respective homes. A few minutes later, Paul left and walked home. Am I correct so far?"

Ralph nodded. "Yes, you are absolutely correct."

"OK. In Paul's inside jacket pocket, at the time he placed his jacket on the sofa in the den, were several hundred dollars in cash, some *Very Valuable* tickets, and some Powerball lottery receipts. He didn't check that pocket again until he arrived home, at which point he discovered that the jacket pocket was empty.

"I am asking you to think hard. Did you see or hear anything, no matter how seemingly unimportant, that might help me determine what happened to the contents of that jacket pocket?"

Ralph was silent for several seconds. Then he spoke slowly and confidently. "Amy, I saw and heard absolutely nothing even remotely connected to Paul's jacket pocket. But I am nearly certain about what must have happened. It's happened to me numerous times, and I'll bet it's frequently happened to you too. Paul believes that he put the money, the tickets, and the receipts into his jacket pocket. But he didn't. He put them somewhere else. Sooner or later, they'll be found in the place where he actually put them."

Amy nodded. "Yes, that kind of thing has happened to me. But Paul says he likes to put cash into his jacket pocket as a backup source of funds in case of an emergency."

"I'm sure," Ralph responded, "that Paul intended to put the cash in his jacket pocket. But we all get distracted and don't always put things where we intended to put them. Amy, have you ever heard of Occam's razor?"

Amy shook her head. "No, I haven't. Jerry, have you ever heard of it?"

Her husband nodded. "Yes, I am familiar with Occam's razor. It's a general rule for problem solving. It states that when looking for an explanation for a phenomenon or series of events, the solution with the least complexity is the most likely to be correct, and the solution with the most complexity is the least likely to be correct."

Amy was impressed. "So, Ralph, now you know why I married Jerry." Everyone laughed, and Ralph continued.

"I agree with Occam. The simple explanation is that Paul put the stuff somewhere else. Any other explanation requires assuming stealth and thievery, which makes no sense, given the setting and the value of the missing items. My friends and I are all reasonably well-off. Obviously, my parents didn't do it. And Anna, our housekeeper, has been with us for many years."

"Ralph, I have to tell you that you speak very clearly and analyze things very intelligently. What are you majoring in at Stenman?"

"Political science, with a minor in philosophy. I plan to go to law school after I graduate."

Amy exploded. "Oh my god, oh my god! I majored in political science at CCNY, and I had planned to attend law school until I was hired at Spy4U and changed my mind. May I ask you something that has nothing to do with my investigation, so you can certainly decline to answer, if you wish. What do you think of Donald Trump as a candidate for president?"

Ralph responded without hesitation. "Amy, I'm happy to answer that question. I like Trump; I like him a lot."

Amy shook her head. "Well, Ralph, you just spoiled the whole interview for me! But you just made Jerry's day!" All three people burst out laughing. When they calmed down, Ralph had something to say.

"Amy, I know this may sound like I'm trying to butter you up, but I'm not. I was very uncomfortable about the prospect of meeting with you regarding this situation. But you put me at ease with your way of speaking, your style of questioning and your sense of humor. Now, I almost think of you as a friend."

Jeremy smiled. "Ralph, you just made Amy's day! So you've now made both of our days." More laughter from everyone.

Ralph shook hands with Amy and Jeremy and then exited the classroom.

After Ralph was gone, Amy smiled at her husband. "Well, Jerry, what do you think?"

Jeremy scratched his head. "I know you're gonna eventually inform me that Ralph said something incriminating or revealing in some kind of way, but I detected nothing unusual whatsoever, and I know you're not going to tell me anything until all the interviews are over."

At twelve forty, in marched Michael Pell. He was five foot seven with long light-brown hair, and he wore wire-rimmed glasses. Amy decided he looked like a hippie poet. They both shook hands with Michael, and then everyone sat down. Amy summarized the events of the previous Friday evening, as she did with Paul. She concluded her summary in the same way.

"In Paul's inside jacket pocket, at the time he placed his jacket on the sofa in the den, were several hundred dollars in cash, some *Very Valuable* tickets, and some Powerball lottery receipts. He didn't check that pocket again until he arrived home, at which point he discovered that the jacket pocket was empty."

Michael managed a weak smile. "I know this meeting is necessary because Paul has to live with his father every day, but I wish his father had not decided to make a big issue out of this situation."

"I think I understand what you mean," replied Amy, "but can you expand a bit on that thought?"

"Sure. We five guys became friends here at Stenman. I like Ralph; we all do. I just met his parents, and I like them too. I'm sure Ralph told them about Paul's emptied jacket pocket. His parents undoubtedly know the truth about what happened, Paul knows the truth, and the rest of us guys also know the truth. Why publicly open up this can of worms and endanger all these relationships?"

Amy smiled. "So, Michael, what is the truth?"

"The truth is that the housekeeper stole the stuff out of Paul's jacket. No one else who was there would have even contemplated stealing, let alone actually do it. We were mainly sitting together, eating and drinking. The housekeeper was the one walking around the apartment. And at one point, I clearly remember seeing her go into the den."

"Did you see her leaving the den? How long did she stay in the den?"

"I don't remember if I noticed her leaving the den, so I can't say how long she was in there. But she's the one who had the best opportunity and the best motive. We all know she did it, even if we won't say it out loud.

"And we shouldn't say it out loud. As I told you, it's a can of worms not worth opening. If Ralph's parents decide to terminate the housekeeper's employment, let them do it on their own."

"Why do you say the housekeeper had the best motive?"

"Because she's the one who may be in need of some extra money."

"But she's been employed by Ralph's parents for many years. Why would she suddenly risk everything by removing stuff from Paul's jacket?"

"Maybe her situation has gotten worse lately. Obviously, we have no way of knowing her actual current circumstances."

Amy nodded. "Good points. What are you majoring in, here at Stenman?"

"Psychology."

"Makes sense, based on what you've been saying. I think you'd be an excellent psychologist."

Amy thanked Michael for his assistance. Then Michael departed, and Amy again turned to Jeremy. "Well?"

"Sweetheart, I think you're right about Michael being a good psychologist. But a good psychologist might still steal the contents of a jacket pocket. Other than that perceptive observation, I noticed nothing unusual in the interview."

Amy nodded. "You know, someone who thinks of himself as a good psychologist might be more apt to believe he could get away with stealing from Paul's jacket."

Danny Orland arrived at one o'clock. He was six feet tall, with wavy brown hair and a nice smile. Amy figured he would be very popular with the ladies. After the requisite introductions, Amy again made her presentation, with the usual ending.

"In Paul's inside jacket pocket, at the time he placed his jacket on the sofa in the den, were several hundred dollars in cash, some *Very Valuable* tickets, and some Powerball lottery receipts. He didn't check that pocket again until he arrived home, at which point he discovered that the jacket pocket was empty."

Danny nodded. "Yes, that's what happened, to the best of my knowledge."

"I am asking you to think hard. Did you see or hear anything, no matter how seemingly unimportant, that might help me determine what happened to the contents of that jacket pocket?"

Danny thought for a few seconds, then he shook his head. "I can't say I saw or heard anything that could help you, but I'm pretty sure of what actually happened. Paul thinks he kept those things in his jacket pocket, but he actually put them somewhere else, at home. I'm sure they'll be found there, at some point."

"But we know," Amy replied, "that Paul usually put cash into his jacket pocket when he went out, as an additional backup in case of an emergency."

Again, Danny engaged in quiet contemplation for a few seconds before responding. "Amy, that makes sense, but it doesn't make sense to carry around theatre tickets and Powerball receipts. Here's my best guess. Paul acquired those items on the day of the awards ceremony. He put them in his jacket pocket. Then, when he was at home, prior to going to the college for the ceremony, he emptied his jacket pocket and put all the contents—not just the tickets and receipts—into a drawer or the like.

"So the cash is currently in a drawer at home, along with the other stuff. It's the kind of thing people do all the time without thinking about what they're doing, and it's easy to forget that you put the cash, plus anything else, into the drawer.

"When Paul got back home from Ralph's apartment and realized his jacket pocket was empty, he knew the cash was supposed to have been there, so he assumed the contents of the pocket had been stolen at Ralph's apartment when, in fact, he had removed everything hours earlier."

Amy smiled. "That's quite an analysis. Are you a psychology major, like Michael? You sound like a student of human nature."

"No, I'm majoring in English. I want to be a journalist."

"Well, anyhow, your scenario could easily be correct. I myself am certainly absentminded, on many occasions, regarding where I put things. While you were at Ralph's apartment, did you happen to notice anyone entering the den before you guys went there to take your jackets and go home?"

"No, but I guess I probably wouldn't have been aware of it if someone did."

Amy and Danny shook hands, and Danny left the room. Jeremy didn't wait for his wife to ask him; he spoke immediately. "Sweetheart, to answer the question you were going to ask, I didn't detect anything unusual or incriminating. But your presentations of the events of a week ago are getting quite boring."

Amy laughed. "Yes, but when I make the presentation to an interviewee, it's the first and only time he's hearing it."

"I was just kidding, but I'm glad there's only one interview left."

The final interviewee, Carmine Toro, arrived as scheduled at one twenty. He was five foot nine and quite a bit overweight. He was wearing gym clothes, complete with sneakers.

Carmine shook hands with Amy and Jeremy and immediately apologized for his attire. "I was at the exercise club meeting between noon and one o'clock, and at that meeting, we tried out various exercises. So I'm dressed accordingly."

Amy smiled and nodded. "No problem. I once had to interview a guy who was virtually naked." Everyone laughed, and Jeremy was trying to decide whether his wife was actually telling the truth.

Amy began her presentation, ending with the lines that her husband had almost memorized, word for word.

"In Paul's inside jacket pocket, at the time he placed his jacket on the sofa in the den, were several hundred dollars in cash, some *Very Valuable* tickets, and some Powerball lottery receipts. He didn't check that pocket again until he arrived home, at which point he discovered that the jacket pocket was empty. Am I correct so far?"

Carmine nodded. "Yes, you are correct. And, Amy, I'm going to make your investigation very easy. I know the housekeeper removed the money and the tickets from Paul's jacket pocket. Case closed."

"How can you be so certain?"

"First of all, from the time we came into Ralph's apartment that evening, I didn't like the looks of that woman. I said to myself that she was going to steal something. And then, while we were having our desserts and drinks, I saw her go into the den. I saw her glance around before entering, to see if anyone was watching her. I guess she didn't notice me watching."

"How long did the housekeeper stay in the den?"

"I'd say about a minute, two at the most. And I observed a furtive look on her face when she left the den."

"But the housekeeper has been working for Ralph's family for many years. She wouldn't risk everything at this point by stealing items out of Paul's jacket pocket, would she?"

Carmine laughed. "How do you know that the housekeeper hasn't been stealing things for years but just hasn't been caught until now?"

Amy laughed. "You know, that's a good point. But it's not a safe move for a housekeeper to rob stuff from a guest's jacket pocket. It's pretty likely to be discovered, maybe even while the guest is still at the apartment."

"You're right, but maybe the housekeeper's personal circumstances changed recently for the worse, and she became desperate and was willing to take a greater risk. By the way, she actually made off with quite a bonanza. Aside from the several hundred dollars, she could probably sell the tickets for additional cash, and then one of the Powerball slips could have turned out to be a winner, maybe even a big winner, who knows?"

"Carmine, you make a clear and cogent argument. You have indeed been a great help to me in my investigation. Thank you so much." Carmine shook hands with Amy and Jeremy, and then he departed. Now Jeremy spoke up.

"Sweetheart, finally I think I do have an observation to make. Two of the four friends saw the housekeeper go into the den. Carmine timed her den visit as one minute, maybe two. That's more than enough time for her to go through several of the jackets and remove the money and tickets from Paul's inside jacket pocket.

"As Michael pointed out, the housekeeper had the best opportunity of anyone there. Her personal circumstances may have given her a motive. So I'd say she should be your prime suspect."

Amy smiled at her husband. "So you're not impressed that Anna—that's her name—has been working for Ralph's family for many years?"

Jeremy shook his head. "Not really. Michael, and especially Carmine, gave good explanations to minimize that argument. So do you agree with me about Anna?"

Amy stroked her husband on his cheek. "You are, indeed, a very thoughtful, logical boy. And I would strongly suspect Anna, except for one thing. I already know which one of Paul's four friends stole the contents of his jacket pocket."

"What?" Jeremy was in a total state of shock. "You're kidding, right?"

Now Amy resumed the cheek-stroking. "Poor boy! I'm not kidding. I'm ninety-nine percent certain that this one particular friend did it. And you should also know who did it. You were there for all four interviews. So apparently, you were not a very observant boy."

"OK, sweetheart, so lay it out for me. Who robbed Paul's jacket pocket?"

Amy continued the stroking, her voice now getting sexier. "I can see that you're a very inquisitive boy"—Jeremy was now splitting his attention between Amy's words and the rapidly growing bulge in his pants—"so I'll now relieve your tension, I mean regarding the solution to this case.

"Blake was backing a play entitled *Very Valuable*. However, he wanted to remain in the background, and his son Paul was not aware of the title of the play until shortly before the awards ceremony. So certainly Paul's friends were also not aware; why should they be?

"Of course, if one of them stole the contents from Paul's jacket pocket, he would see the two tickets with the name of the play printed on them, as well as the venue, namely, the Stanley Theatre. So the thief would be the only person to recognize '*Very Valuable*' as the name of a theatre play.

"Now, in my presentation to the friends at their interviews, I was very careful to repeat the exact same words each time, namely, that the jacket pocket had contained, several hundred dollars in cash, some *Very Valuable* tickets, and some Powerball lottery receipts.

"Any interviewee who was not the thief would definitely interpret what I was saying as that the tickets were very valuable, meaning, worth a lot of money. This characterization might include some theatre tickets but would also include tickets for sporting events, theme parks, outdoor rock concerts, and so on.

"And yet, one of the four friends specifically referred to the stolen tickets as 'theatre tickets.' This is almost certainly because he knew that when I said '*Very Valuable*,' I was referring to the play. He knew that because he had stolen and looked at the tickets." At his point, Amy stopped stroking her husband's cheek.

"Jerry, you do recall which one of the four friends said 'theatre tickets,' don't you? So who was it?"

He shook his head. "No, I'm very embarrassed to tell you that I don't recall anyone using the word 'theatre' at any time during their interview."

"Well, you were not aware, prior to the interviews, that you should be alert to one of them using that word. I, of course, was. So you can be forgiven for not noticing. It was Danny. He told me that it didn't make sense for Paul to carry around theatre tickets and Powerball receipts."

"Yes!" interrupted Jeremy. "Now I do remember! Danny said Paul probably went to put those items in a drawer at his house but, instead, put all the pocket contents into the drawer and then forgot that he put anything in there."

Amy nodded. "Right, Jerry. Now you remember the whole context. Paul said he'd be waiting for us in the cafeteria. I guess we should head on over."

When they arrived at the cafeteria, Blake was sitting next to Paul at a table for four, and he motioned them over to take the two empty seats. There were no other people in the vicinity of their table, so Amy reported that her investigation was concluded and explained how she had determined that Danny was the thief.

Paul smiled. "I'm not surprised. I've seen Danny shoplift small items from stores. He has a serious psychological problem, and I hope and believe that he'll eventually seek help. I had always suspected that it was him. But I don't plan to tell Danny that I know he did it, although I'll admit I'm glad that I do now know for sure, and I'll be very careful in dealing with him in the future. So, Amy, I'm very grateful to you for solving the theft.

"And, Dad, please don't tell anyone that you know who took the stuff from my jacket. If I change my mind about not revealing who did it, I'll let you know."

"I won't tell anyone," responded Blake, sounding quite angry, "but why didn't you tell me that you suspected Danny? I should have been kept informed about everything connected in any way to the theft. As it turned out, it didn't matter, but I'm very disappointed in you."

Amy decided that she had to step in at this point. "Blake, may I speak to you privately?"

"That's all right," chimed in Paul, "I have to meet someone in just a few minutes, so I'll leave now."

Jeremy knew what to say at this point. "May I excuse myself to use the men's room?" He rose from his chair and walked away. Now Amy and Blake were alone at their table.

"Blake, you hired me to investigate a theft. Maybe I'm not supposed to tell you this, but I feel I have to, as I believe it's a lot more important to you and Paul than this theft case could ever be.

"Paul knows you love him. But it is important for your future relationship with Paul that he should want to share his thoughts, his successes, and his problems with you. For that to happen, Paul must know that you will be encouraging and understanding, that you will recognize his talents and abilities, and most importantly, that you will respect him as the adult he is now.

"Of course, there will occasions which call for strong guidance. But there will be many more occasions which call for praise and empathy. OK, I'm finished."

Blake was silent for about fifteen seconds. He put his hands on his forehead and lowered his head. Finally, he looked up at Amy, who thought she detected a few tears in his eyes.

"Amy, thank you. But I do have one question. There are hundreds of people, including family, friends, and business associates, with whom I am much closer than I am to you. How come none of them has ever cared enough for Paul and me to say what you just said to me?"

Amy was contemplative. "Maybe it's because they *are* much closer to you than I am."

Blake nodded. "That's profound, and you know, you're probably right. Anyhow, the way you solved the theft case reminds me of Johnny Carson. He made everything he did on his TV show look so easy, but it really wasn't easy at all. Nobody else has ever been able to do it as well as he did. Similarly, you made solving this case seem so easy, but no one else could have done what you did.

"I'm going to tell the person who recommended you that they greatly understated your talent. And I'm going to repeat that to Chester."

Amy turned bright red. "Blake, you're very kind. I don't know what to say."

"You don't have to say anything. Please convey a big thank-you to your husband from Paul and me." Blake rose, shook hands with Amy, and strode out of the cafeteria. When Jeremy returned from the men's room, he found his wife sitting alone at the table.

"Sweetheart, what happened to Blake? Did he react badly to your advice regarding Paul?"

"On the contrary, Blake seemed very moved by what I said, and he expressed his gratitude to me for giving him my advice. He told me to convey to you his and Paul's thanks for helping me with the theft case, and then he left."

"I'm sure you'll get a nice bonus for solving the case. What do you think you'll receive?"

"Mr. Murray never talks about money with me until after a case has been concluded. So I expect to hear from him about that on Monday or Tuesday. I have no idea what kind of financial deal he made with Blake, but Mr. Murray did tell me that Blake was willing to pay big bucks."

"Do you realize that you may be getting a big bonus for less than an hour and a half of investigative work? I'm certainly not complaining, but it's amazing!"

Amy smiled. "Yes, but that's not the right way to look at it. It's like the story about the factory manager, one of whose complicated pieces of machinery was on the blink. He called an expert repairman who specialized in that kind of machinery. The repairman showed up, gave a good hard kick to the machine, and it immediately started working properly.

"The repairman then announced that the bill for his services was five hundred dollars. The manager was shocked. 'How can you justify such a high price for five minutes of your time and one kick?' he complained.

"The repairman replied, 'Easy. Twenty dollars for the five minutes and for the physical kick. Four hundred eighty dollars for me knowing where to kick.' The manager was paying big bucks for the repairman's experience and perceptiveness regarding that kind of machinery."

Jeremy nodded. "Sweetheart, that's an excellent analogy."

Amy flashed her husband a sexy smile. "Along the same lines, while I was starting to lay out my solution to the case, I observed that you were exhibiting some additional tension, not related to the case." She licked her lips. "When we get home, I'll spend some time relieving that tension. Although the time and effort I spend relieving your tension is important—and I think I may make sure it takes a long, long time—even more important is my experience and expertise in this activity."

Amy observed that the bulge in her husband's pants had become even larger. "As a matter of fact, we'd better get home as soon as possible. Your tension is clearly reaching an emergency stage." Amy placed her hand on Jeremy's pants, right over the bulge, and kept it there for about five seconds. "Yes, you need immediate expert attention! We've got to leave here at once and take the subway home. I'll phone my secretary and tell her I have to go home early, due to a family crisis that can't wait."

Jeremy was in no condition, at this point, to give an intelligent response. He followed his wife out of the cafeteria.

Saturday, August 20, 2016

Jane Backman was the last of Filip's three former girlfriends remaining to be interviewed. When Amy contacted her, Jane had requested a Saturday meeting, so at ten in the morning, Amy arrived at an IHOP on Broadway, on the Upper West Side. She joined Jane, who was already seated at a table. She rose and shook Amy's hand, and then they sat down. Jane was tall, like Filip's other two girlfriends, but unlike them, she was a brunette.

"So, Amy, you think Tony Capadora is innocent?"

"I do. I've uncovered some substantial evidence that supports Tony's innocence. But as I had told you, I have a serious suspect, who has been photographed by several surveillance cameras where he appears to be following Filip. I don't know his name. Let me show you his photograph." Amy removed the plastic sleeve from her folder and handed it across the table.

"This man had apparently been following close behind Filip, tailing him, on several occasions in the weeks before he was murdered. Do you recognize him? Or have you seen him before, maybe with Filip or hanging out in his proximity?"

Jane studied the photo for a few seconds. "Yes, I think I may recognize this man. I believe he could be the guy who Filip dealt with occasionally with regard to his sports betting."

"So you're saying Filip was betting on sports with a bookie?"

"Oh yes; I got the impression he was a very heavy gambler. I think his primary contact was someone who worked at Acme, his recording company. But this guy showed up a few times when I was there, and they always went someplace where they could talk in private."

"Do you know who Filip's betting contact was at Acme?"

"No, in fact, I don't recall how I found out that Filip had a contact at work. But I'm pretty sure he did have one." She returned the sleeve to Amy.

"Jane, can you tell me about your time with Filip? When did it begin?"

"It began in late September of last year. I waited to meet Filip after he did a show in Greenwich Village. I flashed my sexiest smile, handed him my card—I'm a hairstylist—and told him to come in for a free hairstyling. I assumed he wouldn't phone me, let alone come to the salon where I work, but a few weeks later, he did show up.

"We were hot and heavy for about a month, at which point the way he treated me began to deteriorate. He became more and more disrespectful and thoughtless. Then he hit me. At that point, I immediately told Filip we were through. I think that was about two weeks before Christmas."

"Is there any other information you can provide about Filip that may help me identify the man in the photo or Filip's killer?"

Jane shook her head. "No, I don't think so."

Amy thanked Jane and departed from the restaurant. She arrived home at eleven thirty and discovered a note on the dining-room table reminding her that her husband was playing tennis and would probably get home at around two thirty. Jeremy actually arrived at two forty, and after kissing him, Amy provided the big news. "Jerry, Filip was a heavy gambler, with bookies." She recounted her interview with Jane.

"So, sweetheart, as I now understand it, Filip had a colleague at Acme who procured drugs for him and also a colleague at Acme who connected him with a bookie."

"Yes, Jerry, but the drug guy and the bookie guy could both be the same person."

Her husband nodded. "I guess that's certainly possible. Have you received Eddie's report yet on the fifteen Acme employees' criminal records?"

"No, not yet. But Brad Zelman told me he expects to have the fingerprint results for the first two girlfriends ready on Monday. And now we know why, after two years of making big money, Filip had a net worth of only around forty-five thousand dollars when he died. He gambled the rest of it away."

"Sweetheart, do you seriously believe that any of the three former girlfriends were involved, in any way, in Filip's murder?"

"No, I don't, but they can't be ruled out. And the fingerprints may tell a different story. One thing is for sure. Filip had the bad habit of becoming nastier and nastier to his girlfriends as time progressed, culminating in him striking them. That pattern is now clear and consistent."

"So, sweetheart, Filip was a drug addict, a heavy gambler, and a verbal and physical abuser of women. Swell guy!"

"Jerry, you sure as hell got that right. And you forgot to add song thief."

Monday, August 22, 2016

At 9:45 a.m., Chester asked Amy to come over to his office. When she got there, her boss had a big smile on his face and a check in his hand.

"Amy, I've been told that you broke the speed record in solving Blake's case!"

"Well, I got lucky. I set a trap, and the thief fell right into it."

Chester smiled. "Well, you seem to have been lucky an amazing number of times in recent years." They both laughed. "Anyhow, I spoke to Blake on Friday afternoon, and he transferred your bonus money to our Spy4U bank account. We had not previously negotiated any particular bonus for you solving the case, but Blake assured me that he would do the right thing. As I've known him for some time, I relied on his word. And he came through, in spades. This check is for you."

He reached out his hand, and Amy took the check. She immediately let out a shriek. "Oh my god! Ten thousand dollars, oh my god!"

Chester smiled. "Blake told me to inform you that four thousand dollars is for solving the case, and the remaining six thousand is for caring and having the courage to give him advice on a personal matter. He said to tell you he plans to follow your advice from now on."

"Oh my god, oh my god!"

"Amy, obviously, the bonus Blake is paying you is probably twenty times the value of what was stolen. But Blake is a very wealthy man; for him, the issue was not money but identifying which friend Paul should realize he cannot trust or rely on."

"Oh my god, oh my god!"

"Well, congratulations for a job well done. I asked Blake if he wanted to tell me about your advice. He said no. So I guess I shouldn't ask you."

Amy smiled. "You are correct. You shouldn't ask, and I shouldn't tell." Then she exited Chester's office.

When Amy returned to her office, she found a phone message from Brad. "Hi, Amy, I got some good prints for the two women off the plastic sleeves you gave me, and they do not match the prints from the gun."

Then, at eleven, her phone rang; it was Eddie. "Amy, out of the fifteen names you gave me, I could find no police records of any kind for thirteen of them. There are two who do have records. Dennis Bartow was arrested for possession of cocaine. This was fourteen years ago, when he was twenty. He pleaded it down and got a small suspended sentence. Kevin Franco was arrested for solicitation for prostitution—he wasn't the actual prostitute—ten years ago, when he was thirty. He also ended up with a suspended sentence."

Amy thanked Eddie and then hung up and called her husband. "Jerry, Jerry! I received a bonus of ten thousand dollars! Blake told Mr. Murray that six thousand of that was for the personal advice I gave him!"

"Wow, sweetheart, that's amazing! Congratulations, it did take some amount of courage for you to risk antagonizing Blake by saying what you felt you had to say."

"And, Jerry, guess who are the only two Acme people out of fifteen who have police records." Her husband guessed correctly. Amy then related all the details.

"So, sweetheart, I am assuming you now believe that Dennis was probably Filip's drug pusher."

"Yes, you're correct. However, with regard to the bookie connection, I'm assuming it's either Kevin or Dennis, but I have no idea which one."

"Sweetheart, gambling and prostitution are often run by the same criminal operations, aren't they?"

"Yes, I think so, but that probably doesn't trickle down to low-level criminals, like Kevin, with regard to the soliciting charge. Of course, I'm gonna talk to both of them. I may have enough leverage to get them to take polygraph tests regarding Filip's murder."

"Of course, if one of them is the killer, he will refuse the polygraph."

"Jerry, you're right; the killer will refuse the polygraph, unless he's really dumb. But I hope I can, at the very least, obtain both men's fingerprints. We'll see if I can extract more from them besides prints."

Wednesday, August 24, 2016

At 9:40 a.m., Bart Mallon welcomed Amy into his small office at Acme's headquarters. Bart was five foot ten and somewhat overweight. Amy knew he was thirty-two years old and was employed by Acme as a musician. They took seats on opposite sides of Bart's desk.

"Amy, I was very surprised when you phoned and told me you're pretty sure that Tony Capadora did not murder Filip."

"Well, I have unearthed some substantial evidence which strongly points to Tony's innocence. However, as I mentioned, I have a surveillance photo of a man who is now one of my prime suspects. He is in the act of walking a few steps behind Filip. There is additional evidence of him tailing Filip for a period of time.

"I need you to examine his photograph to see if you recognize this man or if you may have ever seen him with or near Filip. It would be even better if you can provide his name."

Bart took the sleeve from Amy and stared at it, silently, for about ten seconds. Then he responded confidently. "No, I'm pretty sure I've never seen this man before." Bart returned the sleeve to Amy. "By the way, can you tell me what evidence you have uncovered that shows Tony is innocent?"

"Bart, I wish I could, but due to protecting confidential informants, I can't reveal anything at this time. Now, I would appreciate it if you told me about yourself and Filip, with regard to Karen Maddox."

Bart nodded. "Yeah, I figured you'd get to that. I really liked Karen. I thought we had something special going on. So, naturally, when, out of the blue, she split up with me and started seeing Filip, I figured he made a play for her and stole her from me.

"It took some time, but I came to realize that Karen was giving me signals, all along, that she wasn't as happy in our relationship as I was. Also, two people have told me that they observed Karen coming on to Filip more than a week before she broke up with me. So I have accepted that there was never a chance of anything permanent between us."

Amy nodded and smiled. "I'm very happy to hear that you are now free of bitterness and jealousy, with regard to Filip. Is there anything else you can tell me that may help me discover who killed Filip?"

"No, I don't think so. I didn't do any of Filip's soundtracks. Morton did call me in originally, when he received Filip's CD in the mail. I listened, and the only song I liked at all was 'I'll Never Believe It.' Actually, I liked that song a lot, and Morton agreed with me.

"Beyond that, I wasn't involved too much with Filip, professionally. However, I will definitely call you if I think of something else I can tell you."

They shook hands, and Amy went outside for a stroll before her scheduled ten-thirty interview with Dennis Bartow. She decided she had to play the percentages and go all in.

Dennis was employed by Acme as a sound engineer, and Amy met with him in the recording room, which was not being used at the time, so they were alone. Dennis was five foot ten and thin. He was prematurely balding.

"Amy, I was very intrigued when you contacted me and said you have evidence that Tony is innocent. Can you elaborate?"

Amy gave Dennis the same presentation she had given for her previous interviews. Then she handed the sleeve to Dennis, who briefly studied the photo.

"No, I'm sorry to tell you that I don't remember ever seeing this man." He gave it back to Amy. "You really think there's a good chance this guy killed Filip?"

Amy nodded. "Yes, there is some other evidence, in addition to the surveillance photos." Amy knew it was now or never. She went with now. "Now, Dennis, we have to discuss Filip's purchases of illegal drugs."

She immediately detected a brief look of absolute horror on her interviewee's face. At that moment, Amy knew she had her man.

"My firm, Spy4U has amassed a large amount of evidence regarding Filip's purchases of illegal drugs. But we weren't hired to uncover a drug pusher. We were hired to uncover a murderer. So Spy4U will not reveal our evidence regarding drugs to the authorities unless I tell them that it's necessary to help us solve the murder case. And if you will help me out, I am almost certain that it will not be necessary.

"I would like you to take a lie detector test, administered by Franklin Sorel. He is the best in the business. His office is in Midtown Manhattan. He will ask you if you were involved in Filip's murder. He will also ask if you know anything about who was responsible for the murder. He will definitely not ask you anything about drugs." Dennis breathed a clearly audible sigh of relief.

"I also have to ask you whether you aided Filip in any way with regard to illegal sports betting."

Now there was no visible discomfort on his face. Dennis shook his head. "Absolutely not."

"So is it OK for Mr. Sorel to also ask you about that on the polygraph?"

"Sure. So the polygraph is only about the murder and the sports betting, right?"

"Right, and if you pass the polygraph, we will make every effort to keep our drug findings completely confidential. I need you to take the polygraph by tomorrow at the latest. Preferably do it today, after work, if possible. Mr. Sorel will rearrange his schedule to expedite the test."

"OK, I'll take the polygraph. And, Amy, thank you for…well, you know what I mean. I guess you also know about what happened to me fourteen years ago, right?"

Amy smiled and nodded. "Yes, I'm a very good detective. Suspended sentence."

Dennis now smiled, for the first time in the interview. "Yes, Amy, for sure, you are a very good detective." Amy gave Dennis all the necessary information regarding Franklin. Then she left the Acme building and phoned Franklin to tell him that Dennis would be coming.

Franklin was, of course, as always, delighted to hear from one of his very best clients. "Amy, you do want me to expedite, regardless of the extra fee, right?"

"Right. This evening would be perfect, otherwise tomorrow." Amy detailed the questions she wanted Franklin to ask Dennis on the test, as well as the contact information.

"Amy, I'm so grateful that you want me to expedite. I need you now more than ever! My wife strongly hinted yesterday that I should give her a diamond necklace for Labor Day."

"Labor Day?"

"Yes, she says that the holiday was originally intended to honor women giving birth." Amy burst into laughter, and then they hung up.

Amy arrived home at five, and after dinner for two, consisting of a large pepperoni pizza with meatball and mushroom toppings plus chocolate ice cream for dessert, she related to Jeremy the morning's developments at the Acme office.

"So, Jerry, if Dennis passes the polygraph—which is certainly not guaranteed—we'll be pretty sure that Kevin was Filip's bookie connection."

Her husband nodded. "I agree. Of course, there's also the fingerprints. Obviously, I assume that if Dennis passes the polygraph, his prints will not match those on the gun."

"That's overwhelmingly likely, but not absolutely guaranteed. Theoretically, Dennis could have a mental disorder and believe he didn't kill Filip when he actually did. Then he would pass the polygraph while still being the murderer. Of course, I wouldn't bet on that, but I would definitely say that fingerprints trump polygraphs—now why in hell did I have to use that ugly word?"

"What word?"

"Jerry, you know damn well what word I'm talking about, and I'm not going to use it again."

He smiled. "Oh, *that* word, my new favorite word!"

"Well, after Election Day, you'll have to find a different new favorite word."

"You may indeed be right about that; we'll have to wait and see. So, sweetheart, what is your current favorite word?"

His wife was quiet for about ten seconds, deep in thought. Then she smiled. "I know what you're probably thinking it is. But if so, you would be wrong. I would say my current favorite word is definitely *bonus*!" They both burst out laughing.

At seven thirty, her phone rang. "Hello, Amy, it's Franklin." She put on the speakerphone. "I am so grateful to you, and so is my wife. My polygraph appointment with Dennis Bartow was at six o'clock. That means my normal fee is doubled. Anyhow, I am very confident, based on the results, that Dennis was not involved in Filip's murder, does not know who did it, and had no gambling connection of any kind with Filip."

Amy thanked Franklin and hung up. "So, Jerry, you heard. It looks like Dennis is no longer a suspect."

"But, sweetheart, you still submitted his fingerprints to Brad, right?"

"Of course, that goes without saying."

Friday, August 26, 2016

At twenty-five past noon, Amy entered the Northside Diner, a few blocks from the construction site where Oscar Banks was currently employed. She had previously phoned Oscar and offered to treat him to lunch. Amy took a seat near the entrance and had only a five-minute wait. A six-foot-two hunk of a man, with a sleeveless shirt revealing his massive, muscular arms, walked through the entrance and almost immediately stared at her, up and down. He appeared to be in his late twenties. He walked to where Amy was sitting.

"You must be Amy, I'm Oscar." They shook hands and were seated in a booth by the hostess. Oscar ordered a massive amount of food and an expensive wine. Amy ordered a burger and a Coke Zero.

"Oscar, as I had mentioned, I have uncovered strong evidence which indicates that Tony Capadora is actually innocent of killing Filip. I have a surveillance photo of a man who appears to have been following close behind Filip. I don't know his name, but we have reason to believe he was tailing Filip, more than once. I would like you to examine the photo and tell me if you recognize him and whether you ever saw him with Filip or at the Acme headquarters." Amy handed Oscar the plastic sleeve containing the photo.

After staring at the photo for a few seconds, Oscar responded. "No, to the best of my recollection, I never saw this man before." Oscar handed the sleeve back to Amy. "And Amy, please don't take offense, but I have to ask. Are you married or in a serious relationship?"

Amy smiled. "Of course, I'm not offended. I'm very happily married, but thank you for the compliment. However, I would think you'd have very little difficulty attracting a young lady."

"Yes, but ladies seem to be interested in me for the wrong reason. And therefore, they turn out to be the wrong ladies for me."

Amy laughed. "I can imagine the reason why some women might be interested in you. Can you tell me about the dispute you had with Filip?"

Now Oscar laughed. "Yeah, I assumed you'd be asking me about that. Hey, look, I freely admit it; I behaved like a total jerk. I was terminated by Acme only a few weeks after they signed with Filip and brought him to this country.

"I had a bad feeling about Filip as soon as I saw him. I thought his 'sexy' looks were highly overrated. The same for his singing voice. I'll admit that his hit song, 'I'll Never Believe It,' has a catchy melody. But that was a fluke. All of Filip's other musical compositions stink. And don't tell me about 'It's Not in My Power.' I'll bet Tony was telling the truth, and Filip stole that song from him.

"So I let my bitterness about being fired and my intense dislike of Filip take the place of logical thinking. Never mind that there was no fixed maximum number of singers that Acme could work with. Never mind that my songs weren't selling, and I was hardly ever being booked for live performances. I decided that Acme had dumped me in favor of Filip.

"It wasn't too convenient for me to take my anger out on Acme, but it was easy to take it out on Filip. I insulted him in front of other people, and on my last day at Acme, I almost attacked him, physically. Luckily, someone stepped between us.

"Now, I realize I behaved very badly, with no justification. I wish I could personally tell Filip I'm sorry, but unfortunately, he was murdered. However, when you get a chance, please convey my sincere apology to Morton and everyone else at Acme."

Amy nodded. "I will convey your apology, and I know it will be appreciated. Can you think of anything else you can tell me, no matter how minor, regarding Filip, that I might be able to use to help uncover his killer?"

"No, I don't think so, but I'll call you if I think of something."

They spent the rest of the meal discussing what kind of women Oscar should be interested in dating. Eventually, Amy paid the check, shook hands with Oscar, and returned to Spy4U, where she checked her messages and e-mails, and then called her husband.

"Jerry, I received a message from Brad, which he sent only a few minutes ago. All the prints I've submitted failed to match the prints on the murder weapon. And there were a decent number of good prints from each of my suspects. Of course, he hasn't looked at Oscar's prints yet, as I've just interviewed Oscar."

"So, did Oscar say anything interesting?"

"Not really. He wants me to tell Morton and the other Acme people how sorry he is for throwing tantrums when he was fired and for saying Acme dumped him to go with Filip. He now realizes that there was no connection between Filip being hired and him being fired."

"Do you believe Oscar, or was he just performing for you?"

"I don't know. He seemed sincere."

"Just remember this. If Tony didn't kill Filip, then somebody else did. What will you do when you've interviewed everyone, all seem sincere, and none of their prints match up?"

"Jerry, again I can only say I don't know. And I will, indeed, run out of people to interview pretty soon. I keep having this feeling that I'm missing something very important."

"Sweetheart, do you think there's a chance that some lowlife with no connection whatsoever to Filip walked into the Acme office and shot him?"

"I greatly doubt it. Filip was shot four times, which makes me think the killer had a really serious grudge against him. Also, Detective Oteri told me nothing was stolen from Filip or Acme. Of course, the killer could be a mentally unstable nut who walked in, shot Flip four times just for the fun of it, and then walked out. But here's the biggest reason why your idea doesn't stand up: why would such a killer hide the murder weapon in Tony's backyard?"

Jeremy smiled. "Well, you've convinced me. But then it means one of these 'sincere' people is probably the killer."

Amy nodded. "Yep, and so far, I've got nothing. Well, as Mr. Murray has told me several times, all I can do is my best."

Saturday, August 27, 2016

At 1:10 p.m., Amy Bell and Denise Bromfield were enjoying girls' lunch out at Cal's Coffee and Cake in Greenwich Village. Jeremy was busy playing tennis, and Denise's husband was busy finalizing a lengthy article he was writing for an academic journal, to beat a rapidly approaching deadline.

Amy told anybody who would listen that Denise was the most amazing woman she had ever met. Eight years before, Denise was a beautiful waitress who grew up poor and never attended college. But she was a voracious reader, mainly of nonfiction. Denise devoured volume after volume, retaining a great deal of the information the books provided. She particularly enjoyed reading books on business and economics.

Then an enormously wealthy corporate CEO, twice her age, met Denise when she waited on his table. A few weeks later, they were married. When the CEO died, a few years into the marriage, Denise inherited everything and, at the age of thirty, became an extremely wealthy woman. She set up a charitable foundation, Return to Learn, and became its president.

Amy first met Denise while investigating a murder case. During the course of that investigation, Amy uncovered some of Denise's darkest secrets. But all was forgiven, and Amy and Denise had become very good friends.

Amy also played a big role in getting Denise together with her second and current husband, Gary Bromfield, a college professor of Russian history. Denise and Gary lived in a huge co-op apartment on the Upper West Side.

"So, Denise," inquired Amy, "is there any hot topic you and Gary have been discussing, or maybe debating, lately?"

"Well, actually we've been discussing Kazakhstan. There are a lot of political and economic aspects there which are rather complicated and can seriously affect the neighboring countries."

Amy smiled. "You know, that's what I was emphasizing to Jerry just the other day, namely, that he should watch how events in Kazakhstan affect its neighbors." Denise broke into hysterical laughter.

When Denise calmed down, Amy had a question for her friend. "Denise, this came up in a trivia contest, and I'd like your opinion. Given that the southern portion of the Hudson River is half in New York and half in New Jersey and the rest is entirely in New York, is it correct to say that the Hudson River is always in New York State?"

Denise shook her head. "No way! For a river to be always in New York, it would require it is never *not* in New York. As the Hudson is sometimes partially not in New York, it is therefore not always in New York."

"Aha! That's what I said, and the quizmaster, the guy running the trivia, said I was wrong."

"Well, Amy, in this case, I am absolutely confident that you were right."

"One more trivia question. What's the largest lake in the world, in surface area?"

Denise laughed. "It's quite a coincidence that you are asking me this, because the answer is the 'Caspian Sea,' and it's bordered in part by Kazakhstan. Gary and I were, just a few days ago, discussing some serious current environmental threats regarding the Caspian Sea."

"The quizmaster said the correct answer is 'Lake Superior.' I vehemently protested, but he just gave me a dirty look and talked to me condescendingly."

"Amy, 'Lake Superior' would be correct only if they restricted it to freshwater lakes."

"It never ceases to amaze me that you know absolutely everything! We should do trivia contests together, you, me, Jerry, and Gary. I can find some places that run weekly trivia, and we can check them out to see which venue we like best."

"Amy, please don't take this the wrong way, but Gary and I were on the Superior Titan cruise with you and Jeremy, so I am absolutely positive that the one thing I do not want to do with you is trivia."

Amy smiled and nodded. "That's OK, I understand. I sometimes can't control myself when I disagree with what is stated
to be the correct answer. Well, I have another suggestion for
the four of us. There's a singer I interviewed regarding a case
I'm currently working on. Her name is Karen Maddox. She
does a seventy-five-minute performance, in Louie's Lounge at
the Crawford Hotel, at seven thirty and also at ten thirty, five
evenings a week. How about the four of us show up at Louie's
at five thirty on Saturday, a week from today? We can have a
leisurely dinner there and then take in Karen's show. The hotel
is on Seventh Avenue, a few blocks south of Central Park."

Denise nodded. "Sounds great to me. I'll make sure it's OK
with Gary, and I'll call you to confirm. I presume you'll also
have to speak to Jeremy."

Amy smiled. "Yes, but that's just a formality." The two women
laughed, then Denise had a question.

"Amy, what kind of case are you working on that involves
Karen?"

"It's a murder case, believe it or not. But Karen is not a serious
suspect."

"Do you have any serious suspects?"

"My one serious suspect just passed a polygraph test. So now
I have no serious suspects. Have you ever heard of Occam's
razor?"

Denise nodded. "Yes, I have. It says that when trying to determine how or why something happened, look for the least com-

plex explanation. Actually, the name 'Occam' comes from the English Franciscan friar William of Ockham."

Amy laughed. "Of course, you know everything there is to know about Occam's razor. Why did I even ask? Well, in the case I'm investigating, Occam's razor would indicate that the man I'm trying to clear is actually guilty. But I'm convinced he isn't guilty, and he has also passed a polygraph test."

Denise was contemplative. "Amy, you are the genius detective, not I. You see things no one else sees. You solve cases no one else could solve. But I've listened to what you've been saying about your current case, and I have some advice.

"I'm a big fan of Occam, and I'm going to say to you what he'd say. You found the least complex explanation for the murder, which turned out to be incorrect. So there is probably another equally least complex explanation which is the correct one. It may be an explanation stemming from a totally different way of looking at the murder. Find that different perspective, and find the corresponding least complex explanation. Then you will probably be able to solve your case."

Amy smiled. "Denise, that's very profound."

Denise smiled back. "I know!" They both broke into laughter.

Monday, August 29, 2016

Amy took the subway to Woodside and arrived at the Acme Melodies headquarters building at 9:45 a.m. She stopped in to say hello to Morton and, as she had promised, conveyed Oscar's apology for his behavior after he was told he would be terminated. Morton assured Amy that he would tell all his Acme people what Oscar had said.

Then Amy walked down the hall to the office of Barry Garner, the talent liaison. Barry was expecting her; he ushered Amy in and told her where to sit. He offered Amy a drink, and she accepted a Diet Pepsi.

Barry was five foot seven and a bit overweight. He had a nice, friendly smile. Amy knew that Barry was thirty-eight years old and single.

"Amy, ever since the police found the murder weapon in Tony Capadora's backyard, I have assumed Tony was obviously guilty of Filip's murder. You should have seen how agitated Tony was when he came here a few months ago and claimed—without even a shred of evidence—that Filip had stolen his song. He sounded deranged; he probably actually believed the story he was telling us. After Filip brushed him off, I remember thinking at the time that Tony looked like if he could kill Filip right then and there, he would.

"So it was no surprise to me whatsoever when Tony was arrested for the murder. But now you tell me you have new evidence that probably clears Tony, and you have another prime suspect. OK, what evidence, and what suspect?"

"Barry, my evidence is very strong, but there are confidentiality issues. I wish I could present my evidence to you at this time, but unfortunately, I can't. However, I do have a surveillance photo of my new main suspect. I don't have his name, but he's been photographed walking close behind Filip on several occasions. We think he was tailing Filip. Please study the photo carefully." Amy handed the sleeve to Barry. "Can you identify this man, or have you ever seen him with Filip or here at Acme?"

After about ten seconds, Barry responded. "Sorry, I have no recollection of ever seeing this man." He returned the sleeve to Amy.

"Well, thanks for looking at the photo. Now it would be very useful to me in investigating the murder if you would tell me about your time with Filip. Don't skip any details; I never know what small, seemingly unimportant piece of information will turn out to be crucial in solving a case."

Barry nodded. "OK, I was assigned as Filip's talent liaison as soon as he arrived here from Bulgaria. I immediately set up his Facebook account, to which I alone, and not Filip, would have access. Then I helped select Filip's new wardrobe.

"I worked with our music arrangers and our lyrics editor to get Filip's song 'I'll Never Believe It' ready for Filip to do the final recording. I worked with our assistant music producer to choose the other songs—not written by Filip—for his CD.

"Once the CD was released, I worked with our PR people to get Filip into the media and to get radio stations to play 'I'll Never Believe It.'

"Of course, I was always consulting with Morton and acting on his advice."

"I assume," Amy interjected, "that you worked with other Acme talent also."

"Yes, I am one of two talent liaison people here at Acme. So we both are involved with several singers."

"So you worked on arranging Filip's live shows?"

"Yes, and I usually attended his shows. On a few occasions, however, there was a conflict, and I had to be somewhere else. But otherwise, I was there."

"Did Filip have a lot of groupies who wanted to meet him and then possibly have sex with him after the shows?"

"I wouldn't say a lot of groupies, but there were some. Filip actually met one of his former girlfriends, Jane Backman, after one of his shows. Of course, she wasn't a teenager, like most of them."

Amy nodded. "I spoke to Jane. She gave Filip her business card, and he came to her beauty salon a few weeks later."

"Yes, that's accurate. I tried to keep the groupies away from Filip, especially the teenagers. He didn't have sex with any groupies backstage on my watch. I did see some teenagers hand him cards, and he might have possibly contacted one or more of them at a later time."

Amy smiled. "So he might have had backstage sex with a groupie on the occasions when you had to miss his performance."

"Yes, that is possible."

"Do you have the names of any problematic groupies who were bothering Filip?"

"Just one, Anita Groverson. She's nineteen and lives in Elizabeth, New Jersey. And she made it a point to emphasize that she has her own apartment." Amy laughed. "After she showed up at several performances and bothered Filip afterward, I told her to stay away from him."

"Did she stay away?"

"Yes, I never saw her again. But I can't swear that she never contacted Filip in some way."

"Did Filip ever appear to be under the influence of drugs?"

Barry nodded. "Yes, occasionally, but definitely not when he was performing. I warned him about the dangers of using drugs, but I wasn't his guardian, and as you know, drugs proliferate in the entertainment industry."

"Was Filip gambling on sporting events?"

"Yes, and you seem to know all the right questions to ask. You know, I'm sure there are many good detectives, but you are both a good detective and damn good-looking too. Are you, by any chance, single and available?"

Amy smiled and noted that her wedding ring was covered by her writing pad. "I've been very happily married since 2010. But thank you very much for the compliment."

Barry looked disappointed. "OK, well, anyhow, Filip was a big sports bettor. He used a bookie; I never inquired about the bookie's identity. He certainly was earning enough money to be able to afford that vice, and it didn't affect his job performance, so it didn't bother me."

"I heard that you received five thousand dollars as a beneficiary in Filip's will."

"Yes, his friend in Bulgaria and I were the only individual beneficiaries; the rest went to charity. I was very touched that Filip thought of me as his good friend. And actually, I think I was a good friend to Filip. I liked him, and business aside, he had a rags-to-riches story. I very much wanted him to continue to succeed."

"By the way, do you think that Filip stole the song 'It's Not in My Power' from Tony?"

"After seeing what a nutjob Tony was, and his total absence of evidence, I seriously doubt it. Almost all of Filip's song compositions were pretty lousy, but he had the persistence to keep on writing songs, and finally, he came up with a big winner with 'I'll Never Believe It,' which has a great melody. So why couldn't he come up with a second great song? And if Filip had lived, he would eventually have had a third and fourth winner, and so on, given enough time.

"You know, persistence is a big factor for success in life. Don't give up, keep trying. There's a wonderful joke I heard that beautifully illustrates this very serious point. There's this man, Joe Smith, who is not physically attractive. And he doesn't have a lot of money. But Joe has an amazing record of scoring one-night stands with women. Friends have seen him escorting some of these women out of his house the next morning.

"So one of his friends finally asks Joe for the secret of his success with women. 'Well,' he says, 'when I see an attractive woman at a supermarket, a drugstore, or on the street, and she appears not to be wearing a wedding ring, I approach her and tell her that my name is Joe Smith, I find her very attractive, and I would be very appreciative and honored if she would spend the night with me at my house.'

"The friend is dumbfounded. 'What? Don't the women slap you in the face or call you a perverted jerk or just walk away?' Joe responds, 'Yes, most of them do.'

"And there's the moral. You don't need to score big most of the time. You only have to score big a few times—or maybe even only once—to succeed in life."

Amy smiled. "Barry, I like that joke. And it makes an excellent point about persistence, which is also true when doing detective work. There have been several cases where it looked like there was no hope for me to solve them, but I just kept on digging and eventually succeeded."

With that, and after the final pleasantries, the interview ended. After Amy arrived at Spy4U, she phoned her husband. "Jerry, have you heard the joke about the ugly guy who was a big success in getting women to have one-night stands with him at his house—"

"Most of them do!" interrupted Jerry while laughing. "Most of them do! It's a very old joke."

"So how come I never heard it before Barry Garner just told it to me?"

Her husband laughed again. "Because it's typically a joke men tell to each other. But I have heard various less potentially offensive versions of the joke. Recently, I heard a version which involved Aristotle Onassis, believe it or not, before he became rich, going door to door in Argentina, trying to sell tobacco."

"Well, Jerry, now I know the joke, and it's a good one. Anyhow, Barry is one hell of an asset for Acme. He is involved with everything regarding the singers he handles. He builds up close relationships with these people. I can see why Filip remembered Barry in his will."

"So did Barry keep the groupies away from Filip?"

"Mainly, yes, but Barry admits that there were a few performances where he couldn't attend, and Filip would have been free to have sex backstage with a willing groupie. And Barry mentioned one groupie, Anita Groverson, who pestered Filip after his shows, to the extent that Barry told her to get lost."

"Did she actually get lost?"

"Yes, as far as Barry is aware. Anita lives in Elizabeth; I think I'll try to talk to her. She shouldn't be too hard to locate. After all, how many Groversons are there in Elizabeth?"

"Do you view Barry as a serious suspect?"

"No, but of course, I'm sending to Brad the plastic sleeve with his prints. All the evidence indicates that Barry was the best friend Filip had in the United States. Filip thought so much of Barry as a friend that he left Barry five thousand dollars in his will. And if Filip had lived, Barry's professional reputation would have grown as Filip's success grew."

"So who's next on the interview agenda?"

"Kevin Franco. He's the other guy, besides Barry and Dennis, who Filip phoned most frequently. Also, he is the only Acme employee, besides Dennis, who has a police record. As I have already told you, I think he's a very good bet to have been Filip's Acme connection to the bookies. Of course, if you are a big bettor, the bookies want you alive, not dead. Even if you are behind in payments, you might get beat up, but it's very unlikely you'd be killed."

"But Amy, as I've pointed out previously, Filip did get killed, and someone murdered him."

"Yep, I'm probably missing something. I keep thinking about what Denise said. I have to find a different perspective, another way of looking at the murder. Then I should look for the least complex explanation while viewing the murder in that new perspective."

"Sweetheart, I'm not totally sure what all that means."

Amy smiled. "Neither am I, at least not yet."

Tuesday, August 30, 2016

At ten in the morning, Kevin Franco and Amy Bell took seats in the recording room at the Acme headquarters. Kevin was a studio musician, doing backup for Acme's performers. He was five foot ten, with long brown hair and a mustache. Acme decided he looked like a rock musician.

"Amy, when you phoned me you said you wanted to show me a surveillance photo of a suspect in Filip's murder. So you think Tony didn't do it?"

Amy went through her phony story and gave Kevin the sleeve with the photograph. He spent very little time looking at it and then shook his head and returned the sleeve to Amy. "No, I've never seen him before."

"Are you sure?"

"Well, I can't be sure that I've never seen him, but I definitely don't remember him."

"OK, can you tell me about your relationship with Filip?"

"Sure, I did backup music for his recordings. I play various types of guitars, plus I can also do keyboard. For his CD, every song on the CD, except for 'I'll Never Believe It,' was new to Filip. We couldn't use any of his other compositions, because, frankly, they were pretty lousy. So Filip and I worked together for each song so that both of us could learn and perfect our performances."

"Did you also back him up during his live shows?"

"Sometimes. On other occasions, I was backing up another Acme singer's show, so Acme had to hire someone else in my place."

"Is there anything else you can tell me about Filip that might assist me in my investigation?"

"Well, Filip was popular with women. He had several girl-friends—not at the same time—and in between, he was briefly with various women."

"Do you recall any of these women in particular?"

"Just the girlfriends. But I was told one reason Filip lost his girlfriends was that he physically struck them. I once asked him about that. He replied that he sometimes lost control and did things he deeply regretted immediately thereafter, and he knew he had to work on that."

"Did he attend counseling, or do something else, to try to change his pattern of violent behavior toward girlfriends?"

"Not to my knowledge."

"Is there anything else you want to tell me about Filip?"

Kevin shook his head. "None that I can think of."

"Are you sure?" Amy stared into Kevin's eyes. He was clearly now becoming uncomfortable.

"My company, Spy4U, has all sorts of resources to help me gather information and, if necessary, provide it to the police. I have some information about you and Filip, and I hope you will provide the full details so that I do not have to go to the police. I'm going to give you an opportunity to speak now. You may not get another chance." At this point, Kevin was sweating and fidgeting in his seat. He appeared ready to surrender. Amy decided this was the time to go in for the kill.

"When we present our evidence to the police, they will obtain a warrant for your phone and computer records. Some people you've phoned may be very angry with you, knowing that because of you, the police have discovered their involvement."

Kevin capitulated. "OK, I took sports bets from Filip and passed them up the chain. I have a family. My wife has medical problems. I need extra money. No one was hurt. Please don't ruin me. I'll tell you everything I know."

"Well, first, there was another man who sometimes went to see Filip about betting. Who is he?"

"I don't know his real name, but he calls himself Ace. He is the next step up the chain from me. I used to bet sports through Ace until I got married and quit gambling cold turkey. Ace only came to see Filip to settle up things for the week when I was out of town, which is fairly frequently, as I do backup for live performances around the country. I don't have the name or contact information for anyone else up the chain."

"Was Filip ever unable to pay his weekly gambling debt in full?"

"Of course not. He was making great money. He always paid promptly and in full. Of course, sometimes we paid him. That's why no one was hurt. It was a victimless thing. I made money, which I really needed, and Filip had fun.

"And just so you'll know, on the weekend of the murder, I was in Seattle, backing up one of Acme's singers, for live performances on Friday evening and on Saturday afternoon. I can prove it."

"OK, Kevin, I need you to take a polygraph test to verify that you had no connection to the murder, you don't know of anyone who had any connection to the murder, and to your knowledge, Filip never failed to pay his entire debts on time. There will be no questions regarding illegal sports betting. My polygraph man, Franklin Sorel, is in Midtown Manhattan. I'll give you his contact information. I want you to take the test as soon as possible, definitely by tomorrow.

"If you pass the polygraph, my company and I will do everything we can to keep our information absolutely confidential, with no police involvement."

Now Kevin looked relieved. "Yes, I'll take the polygraph."

"Fine. How many children do you have?"

"Two, a girl and a boy."

"Well, I hope your wife regains her health." They shook hands, and Amy departed.

At five fifteen, Amy joined her husband for dinner at Dario's Italian Restaurant, a few blocks from their apartment. She updated him regarding Kevin.

"Franklin called and told me Kevin will be taking his polygraph test this evening at six thirty."

"Sweetheart, given Filip's income for the past year, it seems very likely that Kevin was telling the truth and Filip always paid on time. So where could there be any motive for murder?"

"Yeah, I'm pretty sure that Kevin will pass the test on all questions. And you're right. As we had discussed, even if Filip was not paying what he was supposed to, it's not likely he would be murdered. But if he always paid his debts on time, then there is absolutely no motive at all."

So whom are you left with?"

"Well, I managed to locate Anita Groverson; I'm meeting her for lunch on Thursday. And she is currently the last interviewee on my list. By the way, when I was having lunch with Denise at Cal's last Saturday—"

"Oh my goodness," interrupted Jeremy, "Cal's, that sure brings back a lot of memories!" He was referring to Cal's being significant in Amy's first murder case, which she called the Teacher's Pet case.

Amy smiled. "You bet! Anyhow, I asked Denise if she would be interested in the four of us competing in trivia contests as a team, and she politely declined."

"Denise is a very smart woman!"

"OK, don't rub it in. So that's when I suggested we go to the Crawford Hotel this coming Saturday to have dinner and see Karen sing. I mentioned it to you previously, and I just want to remind you not to play tennis too late on Saturday afternoon. You should definitely be home by three."

Jeremy smiled. "Don't worry. Jason and I are already reserved for tennis between ten and noon. And isn't it more correct to say '*hear* Karen sing' rather than '*see* Karen sing'? After all, you don't see a song."

"Yes, but you do see the singer."

There were a few seconds of silence, then Jeremy nodded. "You have a point. Let me think about it for a while."

At eight o'clock, Franklin phoned. "Amy, Kevin Franco took the polygraph test this evening and based on the results, I am very confident he was telling the truth in all his responses." Amy thanked Franklin and hung up.

"Well, Jerry, it's Anita or bust—pardon the double entendre." They both burst out laughing.

Thursday, September 1, 2016

At quarter past noon, when Amy Bell arrived at the Elmora Eatery, in Elizabeth, Anita Groverson was waiting for her outside the entrance. She was five foot six and had a very cute face—at least in Amy's opinion—and long brown hair. Also, she was, to use a term Amy sometimes used, superstacked. They introduced themselves, entered the restaurant, and were seated in a booth by the hostess.

"Amy, I have to be back at work by one forty-five, so let's mention to the waitress that we have to be done by one thirty. But I have to tell you, I've never spoken to a private detective before, and I'm really excited! I had heard that Filip Beron was murdered; boy, is that a bummer!"

They gave the appropriate instructions to the waitress, placed their orders, and then Amy gave Anita the sleeve with the photograph and went through her fable about the man in the photo.

"So I would like you to examine the photo and tell me if you ever saw this man while you were waiting backstage for Filip to come out after one of his performances. I understand that you were backstage after several of Filip's performances."

"Yeah, I was trying to get Filip Beron on my bang list. But I didn't succeed. And no, I never saw this man in the photo before." Anita handed the sleeve back to Amy.

Amy was confused. "Bang list?"

"Yeah, my list of all the famous people I've banged."

"What does a person have to do to be a candidate for your bang list?"

"Yeah, he has to be a celebrity who's a man. Celebrities radiate power, and I'm sexually attracted to power in a man. Would you like to hear who's already on my bang list? I think it's pretty impressive, given that I won't be twenty years old for another three months, and I didn't start my bang list until I was seventeen."

Amy smiled. "OK, Anita, let's hear some names."

Anita quickly rattled off about twenty names, including several rock stars whose names Amy immediately recognized, as well as a well-known TV newsman, two Major League baseball players, and one congressman. Amy didn't know whether to believe her, but she suspected that Anita was telling the truth.

"That's an impressive list. Why did you give up on Filip?" *And for God's sake*, Amy thought, *please don't begin your answer with "yeah."*

"Yeah, I tried several times to visit Filip in his dressing room after his shows, and then the guy guarding his dressing room door told me to get lost, permanently. Hell, I have standards. I didn't need that kind of crap."

"So you never saw or contacted Filip after the man told you to get lost, right?"

"Yeah, and besides, Filip wasn't really that famous. I had lots of more famous celebrities to try to add to my bang list. Amy, are there any male celebrities you know to whom you could give my name and phone number? I can give you some photos of me in a bikini for you to hand out. But please, no ringers. I want only true celebrities, whose names people would recognize."

"I'm sorry, Anita, but I don't know any male celebrities. However, you seem to be doing very well on your own. May I ask what kind of work you do?"

"Yeah, I'm a receptionist at an exercise center. It's a fun atmosphere, as well as a great way to meet single men who like to keep fit, if you know what I mean."

Amy smiled. "I know what you mean, but those men generally wouldn't be celebrities."

"Yeah, so those men would be candidates for my dating list, as opposed to my bang list. A girl has to have men to take her out to restaurants and shows and things, you know. But don't get me wrong, I'm not a gold digger. My grandfather passed away several years ago and left me nine million dollars, which I'll collect when I'm twenty-one."

Amy nodded. "Well, that's good to hear. Can you tell me if there is anything you saw or heard with regard to Filip that was in any way unusual? Even a seemingly unimportant small piece of information might help me solve the murder."

"Yeah, I really wish I could help you, but I can't think of anything at all that would be unusual or might help solve your case."

Anita spent the rest of their time at lunch expounding about several of the most famous people she had placed on her bang list. At one twenty-five, Amy paid the check and they said their goodbyes.

When she arrived at Spy4U, there was a phone message from Brad. It was brief. "Hi, Amy, none of your suspects' prints match up with the gun. And they all left good prints. Sorry."

She phoned her husband. "Jerry, I just had the weirdest interview I've ever had." She described what had transpired with Anita. "Can you believe that all she could talk about was her voluminous bang list?"

Jeremy responded immediately. "Yeah, yeah, yeah!" Then he started laughing hysterically. Amy was not amused.

"OK, it's obvious that you're in no condition to have a serious conversation at this time. Bring home some Chinese takeout." Then she hung up.

After dinner, Amy updated her husband. "Brad left me a phone message saying that none of the fingerprints match those on the gun. So the only remaining prints for him to check are Anita's."

Jeremy laughed. "Well, we all know that Anita didn't have enough time between bangs to shoot anyone."

Amy nodded. "You're sure as hell right about that!"

"So, sweetheart, is it time to give up on the case?"

"Of course not! Remember what Barry said about persistence. I'm gonna go back and review my notes and recordings for all my interviews to see if there's something I've missed."

"So you recorded all your interviews?"

"Sure, I secretly record all my interviews. It's standard practice for me; I've done it for years."

"Well, I certainly hope you're not secretly recording us in the bedroom."

"Jerry, do you think I'm crazy? We could be blackmailed if someone got hold of such a recording!" They both broke into laughter.

Friday, September 2, 2016

It was two in the afternoon. Amy Bell had been sitting alone at her desk in her office at Spy4U for the great preponderance of the past five hours. She had ordered lunch delivered to her office.

Amy was, again and again, pouring over her notes and recordings for all her interviews with regard to the *Filip Beron* murder case.

She had made an interesting discovery and was trying to figure out its significance. Five people she interviewed had made the same exact observation. This was completely without any encouragement from Amy. She had not asked any question which required them to discuss the topic of their observation.

Of course, this could just be a weird coincidence. But if, as Amy strongly suspected, it had some sort of significance, she wanted to pursue this new direction for the case.

She recalled what Denise had told her. Find a new direction of investigation, and then use Occam's razor and look for the least complex explanation. Amy knew what would be the least complex explanation for the five-time repetition. But it couldn't be correct, could it?

At this point, the phone rang; it was Brad. "Amy, the final fingerprints you sent me also do not match the prints on the gun. So everyone you interviewed left several good prints, but none of them match."

Amy thanked Brad and phoned her husband. "Jerry, the fingerprints were an absolute wipeout. Brad just called and confirmed that the prints from my last hope, Anita, did not match the prints on the gun."

Her husband laughed. "Boy, am I shocked!"

"Ha ha. Of course, both of the prints on the gun could indeed be from prior to the killer acquiring it. So the prints not matching doesn't exonerate any of them.

"However, I have been studying all the interviews, and I've found an extraordinary coincidence. Five people I interviewed said essentially the same thing, without any prompting from me."

"What did they all say?"

"I'd rather not tell you at this point. But I did report to you what everyone said during their interviews, so you could figure it out."

"Sweetheart, that's not fair. You probably had to study those interviews for some time before noticing this coincidence. I only had one chance to hear your report on each interview."

"Of course, you're right; I'm not being fair. I'll tell you what I discovered in good time, maybe even tomorrow. I'm still trying to figure out if the coincidence has any significance in this case."

"Are you using Occam's razor in your thinking?"

"Yes, and where it leads me is pretty wild. Remember, Denise and Gary tomorrow for dinner."

Saturday, September 3, 2016

Louie's Lounge had a great atmosphere for dinner: nice, soft lighting, pleasant recorded music playing, tables not too close together. At 5:30 p.m., Denise, Gary, Amy, and Jeremy were escorted by the hostess to one of those tables. They ordered drinks and appetizers and told the server not to hurry, as they were also staying there for Karen's show, for which there was a fifteen-dollar-per-person extra charge.

Denise, as usual for occasions like this, was dressed in an evening outfit that most people could not even dream of affording. Amy thought that Denise looked absolutely stunning. The outfit complemented her already extremely good looks.

After the drinks arrived, Amy had a question for Gary. "Denise told me you were writing a major article for a scholarly journal. What's it about?"

"It's about Molotov, the foreign minister of the Soviet Union under Stalin. He was purged from his high Communist Party position by Khrushchev in 1957."

Jeremy smiled. "Is that the Molotov who invented the Molotov cocktail?"

Gary, who had no inkling that this was a joke, responded seriously. "No, the Finns invented the term in 1939, during their war with the Soviet Union."

"So what is your angle in the article?" inquired Amy.

"Basically, it's that Molotov was a lot smarter than most people gave him credit for. By the way, did you guys know that Denise is learning the Russian language?"

"I didn't know," responded Amy. "Denise, why haven't you mentioned it to me?"

"Sorry, I guess it just slipped my mind. Anyhow, we travel to Russia at least once a year in conjunction with Gary's scholarly research, so it just made sense that I should not have to rely on Gary as a translator when we're there."

"Denise," interrupted Jeremy, "I would assume that Russian may be more difficult than languages like French or German, at least with regard to reading and writing, due to the fact that they use a different alphabet than we do."

"The Cyrillic alphabet," volunteered Gary.

Denise shook her head. "No, the Cyrillic alphabet is not a big problem. I got used to it pretty fast."

Amy laughed. "That's because you're so frigging smart. For Jerry and me, the Cyrillic alphabet would be a gigantic problem."

Denise smiled. "I was so hoping, Amy, that you would join me in studying Russian. I'm so very disappointed!" Laughter from all four at the table.

Everyone agreed that the main courses were very tasty. The same for the desserts. Amy loved the chocolate mousse she had ordered, and as soon as she was done, she regretted having eaten it. She mentioned this to the other three, saying that she had sabotaged her efforts to lose weight. All three vehemently asserted that Amy looked perfect as she was and had no need whatsoever to lose weight.

At seven thirty, Karen Maddox began her seventy-five-minute singing performance, accompanied by a pianist. She performed a varied repertoire of songs, from the thirties to the present. Amy felt that Karen had an excellent singing voice.

After the show, Amy came up and congratulated Karen on her performance. "Amy, I recognized you in the audience," said the singer with a broad smile. "I hadn't expected you to come. So thank you for coming."

"Karen, it was our great pleasure—all four of us—and it was a truly enjoyable performance."

When Amy and Jeremy returned to their apartment, her husband was all smiles. "That was a great evening. And Denise never ceases to amaze me. You know, I remember hearing that there is—or at least there was, when I heard about it—one New York City public high school, Staten Island Tech, where students are actually required to study Russian."

Amy was surprised. "You'd think that if you're gonna require an exotic language nowadays, it would be Mandarin Chinese, or possibly Arabic. Of course, those languages also have their own different…"

Suddenly, Amy went silent for twenty seconds. She closed her eyes and appeared deep in thought. "Sweetheart, is everything all right?"

Finally, after another fifteen seconds, she opened her eyes. "Oh my god, oh my god!" Amy raced over to her computer and searched for something on Yahoo. She clicked the mouse and looked at the results for a few seconds. Then she checked something else on the computer for another brief period. At this point, she exploded.

"Yes, yes, yes! On my god! Jerry, what you said at the restaurant solved the case! Oh my god!"

Her husband was dumbfounded. "Sweetheart, I'm delighted to take any credit you wish to give me, but I didn't say anything special at the restaurant. Are you sure the case is solved?"

"Well, I know why the murder was committed, and I can partially identify the killer, but I don't yet have the killer's full name or where the killer can currently be found."

"What? You have solved the case, but you only know part of the killer's name and you don't know where the killer currently is?"

Amy nodded. "Yes, you have it exactly right."

Now Jeremy understood. "Sweetheart, you're joking, right?"

Amy stroked her husband's cheek. "Poor boy! I've solved the case because of what you said, and you don't believe me. You are truly an untrusting boy!"

"OK, so lay it all out for me."

Amy stopped stroking and started her presentation of the solution. "Jerry, I mentioned yesterday that five people I interviewed told me the same thing, unprompted. Well, the five people were Morton, Bart, Oscar, Barry, and Kevin.

"They all told me that in the CD Filip originally sent to Acme, consisting of nine songs he composed, all the songs, except for 'I'll Never Believe It,' were lousy. On the other hand, 'I'll Never Believe It' had a very catchy melody and became a hit.

"We also know that Filip continued to write songs after he arrived in this country, and they were all lousy. He did claim to have written his second hit song, 'It's Not in My Power,' but we now know that, in fact, Tony, not Filip, composed it.

"So, given what I've just told you, I want you to use Occam's razor. What is the least complex explanation for the fact that all of Filip's song compositions were lousy, except for 'I'll Never Believe It,' which was great? This explanation shouldn't have been very hard to figure out. It was there, right in front of us all the time, from shortly after the beginning of my investigation. So, Jerry, have you figured it out?"

Jeremy flashed a broad smile. "Actually, I think I have figured it out. The way you have presented it, the least complex explanation is that Filip actually didn't compose 'I'll Never Believe It.'

Somebody else—someone he knew in Bulgaria—composed it, and Filip stole the song."

"Bingo, Jerry, bingo! Filip did not write 'I'll Never Believe It.' Someone he knew in Bulgaria wrote the song. And Filip stole it from that person, just like he stole 'It's Not in My Power' from Tony. So that actual composer had a motive to kill Filip, and of course, he or she would have had to be in this country on July eighth to have had the opportunity to do so.

"Now let me divert to the major piece of evidence against Tony, besides where they found the murder weapon. I'm talking about the apparent dying declaration by Filip, where he wrote *CAPA* in his loose-leaf, with the last letter tailing off as he died.

"The least complex explanation for this was that Filip was identifying Tony Capadora as the person who had just shot him. But we know that explanation is not correct. So what's the second least complex explanation?

"We had assumed that the second-best explanation was that Filip did not know who shot him but wanted to alert the police that it was probably Tony, who had claimed that Filip stole his song and was enraged.

"But we were wrong. The second least complex explanation is that Filip wrote *CAPA* because he *was*, in fact, able to identify his killer, but *CAPA* referred not to Tony but to someone else."

Jeremy was confused. "How could that reasonably be possible? Are you saying that the killer's name also starts with *CAPA*? That would be incredibly unlikely, and besides, we don't know of anyone, other than Tony, with those four letters in their name, do we?"

"Jerry, you unwittingly gave me the solution at dinner, when you mentioned that the Russians use a different alphabet than ours, namely, the Cyrillic alphabet. I just checked on the Internet. Bulgaria also uses the Cyrillic alphabet. And *CAPA* in Cyrillic corresponds to *SARA* in our alphabet.

"So I am ninety-eight-percent sure that I know what happened, although I may be off on some minor details. Back in Bulgaria, Filip dated a woman named Sarah. She spoke good English and, as a hobby, composed some songs in that language, which she sang for Filip. One of them was 'I'll Never Believe It.'

"The relationship deteriorated over time and ended when Filip began to physically abuse her, as it appears he had done to all his girlfriends. After she broke up with Filip, Sarah disliked him intensely. Imagine her rage when she discovered that Filip was in the United States with a hit song he claimed he had composed but which he had, in fact, stolen from her.

"Sarah traveled to New York this summer, and maybe she confronted Filip about the song, but he brushed her off. Or maybe she didn't contact Filip. In any case, she had seen the stories about Tony claiming that Filip had stolen a different song from him.

"Sarah's rage was now at a peak. One way or another, she procured an illegal gun. Also, she found out that Filip often stayed late and alone at the Acme headquarters. She went there after hours on July eighth and shot Filip four times.

"She knew to frame Tony by burying the gun in Tony's back-yard for two reasons. First was Tony's grudge against Filip. But there was also the TV story, on the following Monday, that Filip had written *CAPA* in his loose-leaf as he died."

Jeremy was not convinced. "But, sweetheart, all the words Filip was writing in his loose-leaf were English words, written in nor-mal English capital letters, not in Cyrillic."

"Sure, but when someone is in a great deal of stress, such as when they've just been shot, they often revert, without even realizing it, to their native language. And also, Filip had undoubtedly written down Sarah's name many times in Cyrillic during the time when they were dating in Bulgaria, so that's the way he was accustomed to writing her name."

Jeremy nodded. "That does make sense. Your solution fits everything perfectly; it looks like you nailed it! But if this Sarah was not in the US on July eighth, then your whole solution collapses."

"That's true, but the reason I'm very confident she was here is that Filip wrote Sarah's name in Cyrillic letters just before he died."

"And I had suggested you might be ready to give up. I'm really ashamed and embarrassed."

"Jerry, you have nothing to be ashamed or embarrassed about. I shouldn't admit this to you, but I will. I made a great speech to you about persistence and not giving up and about Denise's advice. But actually, I was trying to decide how many more days to allow for this case before I gave up and saved Steven Atwood any unnecessary further expenses." They both laughed.

"So now I understand what you said before. You know the killer's first name is Sarah, but you don't know her last name. And you don't know where she is currently. She may currently be at an address in Bulgaria, or she may still be in this country."

Amy nodded. "You got it."

"So what are you gonna do?"

"I'll send an e-mail to Petar Rykov, Filip's Bulgarian friend who received ten thousand dollars from Filip's will. I'll ask Petar if Filip dated or otherwise was acquainted with a woman named Sarah. I'll tell him that if so, I'd like him to tell me about her, and I'd like to phone him at a mutually agreeable time to discuss this.

"Morton told me that Petar was helping Filip with his English, so I presume he can speak and understand enough English to communicate with me. Morton also provided me with Petar's phone and e-mail information.

"As a matter of fact, I'll compose the e-mail right now. Bulgaria time is something like seven hours ahead of us, so I assume he won't read it until he gets up tomorrow morning, his time." Amy went back to her computer and started typing.

"Sweetheart, what if Petar doesn't know this woman named Sarah?"

"Then we could be in big, big trouble, if we want to bring her to justice. But regardless of whether or not I can prove anything, I am ninety-eight percent sure that the case is basically solved, even if we can't locate Sarah or determine her last name."

Jeremy shook his head. "Sweetheart, it's usually you who gets to say this to me, but unfortunately, I have to tell you that you have overlooked the critical issue here. We can both know for sure that this Sarah did it, but without some sort of proof, Tony is still likely to be convicted of first-degree murder and get sent away for life."

"Oh my god, Jerry, oh my god! Of course, you're right. I was so proud of my intellectual achievement in solving the case that I forgot about the person who matters most, namely, Tony. Now, I'm ashamed and embarrassed.

"For now, I can just hope that Petar knows who Sarah is. After all, he was Filip's best friend in Bulgaria, and Filip put Petar in his will. I think there's an excellent chance he can tell me about Sarah. If not, Petar may be able to provide the name of another Bulgarian friend of Filip's who might know about Sarah. Finally, if all else fails, Spy4U may have to retain a Bulgarian detective agency to try to locate her."

Jeremy nodded. "Those are indeed some possible alternatives, but I wouldn't count on them. Your best chance is Petar, far and away."

"Jerry, you're sure as hell right about that!"

Sunday, September 4, 2016

Amy got out of bed early at 6:15 a.m. and checked her e-mails. And there it was, a reply from Petar: "Hello, Amy. Yes, she is Sarah Dimitrov, and she was the best girlfriend Filip ever had. But he ruined it for himself, and she broke it off. Can you phone me at 9:00 a.m., New York time?"

Amy immediately replied, "Yes, I'll phone you at 9:00 a.m., New York time." Then she ran into the bedroom. "Jerry, Jerry! Petar knows Sarah! She is a former girlfriend of Filip's."

"What time is it?" Jeremy looked at the clock. "It's six twenty-five; I need my sleep."

But Amy wasn't going to let her husband sleep. She kept shouting, "He knows Sarah! He knows Sarah!" Jeremy knew the situation was hopeless, so he got up.

At nine o'clock, Petar answered the phone, and Amy put him on the speakerphone. "Hello, Petar, as you know from my e-mail, I am investigating Filip's murder. First of all, I'm very happy that Filip left you ten thousand dollars. I understand you were a very good friend to him."

"Yes, Amy, we were good friends for years. I was thrilled when Filip had his great success in the United States. And I certainly can use the money he left me."

"So you say you know Sarah Dimitrov and she was a girlfriend of Filip's."

"Yes, I lost touch with Sarah in the past two years, but I knew her and spoke to her quite a few times while she was dating Filip. That was during a four-and-a half-month period, starting in the fall of 2013.

"As I told you, Sarah was the best thing that ever happened to Filip, and he threw it all away. Sarah's mother is an American, and her father is a wealthy Bulgarian businessman. They met at university when her father was in America as part of an exchange program. Sarah, their only child, was born in the US, and then the family moved back to Sofia, where her father took a high executive position in the family business. Sarah's father is now running that business.

"So Sarah is an American citizen, with an American first name, including the *h* at the end in the American spelling. Her mother always spoke to her in English, so she's fluent in that language.

"But her mother eventually became unhappy living in Bulgaria. She got a divorce and moved back to New York when Sarah was fifteen. She has since remarried.

"Sarah stayed with her father in Sofia. She went to an expensive private school and then to university for two years. After that, Sarah was given a well-paying, cushy, low-pressure job at her father's firm. Every two years, she flew to New York, where her mother was living, for three months during the summer. The two-year interval was not set in stone. I remember she told me she once visited New York two years in a row.

"Sarah met Filip when they bumped into each other at the post office in late September of 2013. He was not in her social class, but he is a very good-looking guy, and she immediately fell for him, hook, line, and sinker—is that what you Americans say?"

Amy laughed. "Yes, you have an excellent command of American English."

"Thank you, Amy. Anyhow, they had very little in common, except that Sarah had also composed a few songs, but she simply couldn't take her eyes and hands off him. She was in love. Despite their different backgrounds, they appeared to be perfect for each other. They looked so happy together. And then Filip ruined it."

"How exactly did he ruin it?" inquired Amy.

"For some reason I'll never understand, instead of being deeply grateful that he had found a girlfriend like Sarah, he became, over time, more and more angry and disrespectful toward her. Then, in late January, she confided in me that Filip had struck her but he had immediately felt remorse and apologized. She stayed with him until about three weeks later, when she split with him. A few days after that, I met her by chance in a store, and she told me that she ended it right after he struck her for the fourth time. She was quite bitter about the whole thing; all the loving feelings she had for Filip had now been reversed one hundred eighty degrees."

"That's so sad," said Amy in a very sympathetic tone. "Do you know if Sarah visited New York this summer? If so, do you have her home address and phone in New York? Also, do you have that information for her in Bulgaria and maybe an e-mail address?"

"No, as I said, I lost contact with Sarah two years ago. I assume she's still working at her father's company, but I don't know for sure. And I don't have any information about whether she traveled to New York this year. But I have a friend, Rosa, who I think is still friendly with Sarah. I'll phone her now and see if she knows the answers to your questions. Call me back in an hour, OK?"

"Sure, I'll call in an hour. And also please find out if Sarah is married or living with someone."

Amy hung up and smiled at her husband. "You heard everything. Sarah is an American citizen, so she has no trouble coming here and staying for months. Filip became mean to her over time—sounds familiar, right?—eventually hitting her a total of four times, and her feelings toward him changed from love to hate. She composed songs while they were dating. Bingo!"

"Sweetheart, do you think Sarah is still here in New York? Boy, would that be a lucky break!"

"Hopefully, and we'll find out very soon."

When Amy made her second call to Petar, he had the news she was waiting for. "Rosa says all she knows is that this summer, Sarah was scheduled to be in New York for three months, June fifteenth through September fifteenth. She gave me Sarah's address in New York and in Sofia. Rosa also gave me Sarah's cell phone number. She has no e-mail address for Sarah, who, she said, is not married or living with a guy."

"Petar, let me make a wild guess. Sarah is tall and thin and probably a blond."

"Yes! How did you know that?"

"I didn't know, I'm just a good guesser. By the way, do you have a photograph of Sarah?"

"No, but the last time I looked at the website of her father's company, which was over two years ago, Sarah's photo was there. I can give you that website address. Of course, you can also check Facebook."

Petar provided the website address plus the information Rosa had given him. Amy thanked him profusely, and then they hung up.

Amy went to her computer. After a few minutes, she found what she was looking for. "Jerry, the New York address is a two-family house in Kew Gardens, Queens. She's probably renting the smaller, one-bedroom unit, most likely furnished, for a three-month period. At least I hope it's for three months, as in that case, she's still in New York."

Amy then went to the website that Petar had given her. She soon discovered what she was looking for. She printed out the photo and showed it to her husband. "So, Jerry, this is the face of a killer; what do you think of her?"

"I think Sarah is very attractive; she looks like a very sweet girl. I really don't get it. She was born into relative wealth. She's good-looking and has a good job in Bulgaria. I'm sure she could have her choice of boyfriends and eventually find a good husband and have a great life. Why would she travel to New York and murder a former boyfriend, even if he stole her song?"

Amy smiled. "We all understand the power of love; it can make a person do irrational things. But there's also the power of hate, particularly when love turns to hate. For most normal people, unless the object of their hatred has done something truly awful, like a murder, the hatred tends to dissipate over time.

"But I guess that wasn't the case for Sarah. Filip had become mean and had hit her on four occasions, and then she found out that he stole her song. She simply couldn't shake the hatred. It infested itself into her brain and stayed there, constantly bringing itself into her consciousness. The only way she could think of to end the misery this was causing was to kill Filip."

Jeremy nodded. "OK, you've convinced me. But talking about memorable phrases, I think your phrase, 'infested itself into her brain,' is even better than my 'quickie with a groupie!' Anyhow, what are you gonna do now?"

"Well, I've got to find a way to get Sarah's fingerprints. Then I have to pray that one of her prints matches a print on the murder weapon. Otherwise, we're in a familiar situation, namely, knowing the identity of the murderer but being unable to prove it."

"Didn't that circumstance come up in your last murder case?"

Amy smiled as she stroked Jeremy's cheek. "You have a good memory! But at least in that case I found a way to get the culprit sent to prison. In this case, if I can't get a matching print, I'll have to try to come up with some sort of scheme to get Sarah to incriminate herself. But that would be a real long shot."

"You mean, like you successfully did in the Top Prize case, a few years ago?"

Amy resumed stroking. "You have a great memory! I wouldn't have expected that from you. You're such a smart boy!" Her hand moved from his cheek to inside his pants. "For that, you should be rewarded." Amy licked her lips. "As a matter of fact, the time for your reward is right now!"

Jeremy claimed his reward on the living-room rug.

Tuesday, September 6, 2016

At ten fifteen in the morning, Amy was sitting across from Chester at his office desk at Spy4U. "So, Mr. Murray, here's the situation. I have identified the killer of Filip Beron."

"Wow!" Chester interrupted. "Congratulations!"

"Yes, but it's not that simple. The killer is a woman, Sarah Dimitrov, who is an American citizen but lives in Bulgaria. I am not one hundred percent positive that she's currently in New York, but she's supposed to be visiting here for three months, ending on September 15, which is only nine days from today. I have what I believe is Sarah's address. It's a rental apartment in a two-family house in Kew Gardens. I do have her photograph, from a Bulgarian website."

Amy handed her boss a copy of the photo, as well as the Kew Gardens address. "I also know that she's tall, thin, and blond. Sarah assumes that she has gotten away with murder. If she thinks she may be a suspect, she will take the first available flight out of the country.

"To bring Sarah to justice, I need her fingerprints. We can then determine whether one of her prints matches a print on the murder weapon. I need people to do surveillance on her. They should make sure Sarah is unaware of being followed. They must bring back to Spy4U anything she touches that they can take away unobserved. We can check whatever they bring back for fingerprints.

"If Sarah throws something into a public or store trash basket, that might do the trick. That's just one of many possibilities. But again, it's critical that Sarah never realizes that she's being watched."

Chester nodded. "I understand completely. Time is of the essence; we have to act very quickly. But what happens if her prints don't match those on the murder weapon?"

"In that case, unless we can somehow get Sarah to incriminate herself before she returns to Bulgaria, she will get away with murder. And Tony Capadora may well be convicted and go to prison for a long, long time. Of course, I'll tell Tony's attorney the reasons why I'm sure Sarah did it, and he can try to persuade the jury that those reasons constitute reasonable doubt as to whether Tony committed the murder."

"Don't we have an extradition treaty for murder with Bulgaria?"

"Yes, but if there's no matching prints, extradition is never gonna happen. There's just no other hard evidence. I'm not even that confident that Sarah could be extradited if we did have matching prints.

"God, I wish that Acme Melodies had a surveillance camera in or outside their building. That camera would have caught Sarah entering on that evening. And apparently, there were no other surveillance devices on Acme's street. But that's life."

Chester smiled. "Well, Amy, I'll put together surveillance for you, starting tomorrow morning, using only people who have broad experience in picking through garbage." Amy immediately burst into hysterical laughter.

When she calmed down, Amy responded, "Thanks, Mr. Murray. And you certainly have an interesting way of describing certain investigative activities."

"Amy, don't worry, I'll use people who know how to preserve items for possible fingerprints and who know how to observe without being observed."

Amy returned to her office and phoned Jeremy. "Mr. Murray will be setting up surveillance, starting tomorrow morning. My main fear is that Sarah discovers that she's being watched and immediately leaves the country and heads home to Bulgaria before we can obtain any of her fingerprints.

"In fact, even if we obtain some of her prints and they match but Sarah leaves the country before she's arrested, there's no guarantee that she could be extradited from Bulgaria. Time is of the essence."

"Sweetheart, let's just hope that Sarah is still at that address in Kew Gardens and still planning to stay in New York at least until September 15."

"Jerry, you're sure as hell right about that."

Wednesday, September 7, 2016

At 11:25 a.m., Chester phoned Amy at her office with news. "Amy, this surveillance may turn out to have been much easier and shorter in duration than we had ever imagined. At eight thirty this morning, our man, Jake Marliss, observed a woman leaving the downstairs apartment of the two-family house. From the photo and other information you provided, he identified the woman as Sarah.

"Sarah walked a couple of blocks to the Lefferts Diner. Jake followed Sarah in and took a seat near hers. Sarah was dining alone, appeared to be very happy, and was very friendly with the staff, all of whom recognized her and clearly liked her. It appeared from the conversations he overheard that she was a regular, every morning, for breakfast at that diner.

"After Sarah left the diner, Jake walked over, and before the waitress returned to clear Sarah's table, he removed two napkins and one of the two glasses that were there.

"Jake brought this booty back to Spy4U and gave everything to Brad to check for prints. Brad promised to have the results today."

"Oh my god, Mr. Murray. You're right, I never dreamed anything could happen nearly this fast!"

"Well, Amy, now all we can do is keep our fingers crossed."

At three forty-five, Amy's office phone rang. "Hi, Amy, it's Brad. I got a bunch of good prints. Two of those prints match one of the prints on the gun. You got her!"

At three fifty, Jeremy answered his phone. "Oh my god, Jerry, oh my god! We got her, oh my god!" Amy went over all the details.

"Sweetheart, that's absolutely amazing; the whole thing took only a few hours longer than it took you to solve the theft from Paul's jacket pocket!"

"Jerry, we have to celebrate! Meet me at five thirty at Ruth's Chris for dinner. Oh my god, we got her, oh my god!"

Thursday, September 8, 2016

At eleven in the morning, Detective Arthur Oteri welcomed Amy Bell to his office at the Woodside Precinct. "Nice to see you again, Amy. I hope you now realize that Tony Capadora is guilty as charged in the murder of Filip Beron. But I presume you're here to ask me some more questions."

"Actually, Art, it's neither of those two. I would like to identify the murderer for you. Her name is Sarah Dimitrov. She's an American citizen whose home is in Sofia, Bulgaria. However, she is currently here in New York, where her mother resides, for three months, from June fifteenth through September fifteenth. For this period, she has rented the smaller apartment in a two-family house in Kew Gardens. I will provide you with the address.

"Our investigator, Jake Marliss, followed Sarah to the Lefferts diner yesterday morning, and he removed two napkins and a glass from the table where he had been observing her eating breakfast alone. Jake took those items directly to Brad Zelman, Spy4U's fingerprint man.

"Brad found many good prints, and two of those prints matched one of the prints on the murder weapon. We have a complete chain of custody. Sarah to Jake to Brad. So Sarah Dimitrov definitely shot Filip."

Art looked as though he'd just been told that Katy Perry had bench-pressed three hundred pounds. "You're kidding, right?"

"No, I'm not kidding. I'm back here, as promised, with my ten-million-to-one long shot winner." Amy presented to the detective the series of events which resulted in Sarah being identified as the killer.

"Amy, I tip my hat to you. I'll verify what you are telling me about the fingerprints, and if it all checks out, we'll arrest Sarah for murder. I understand she plans to leave the country on September fifteenth—"

"Maybe earlier," interrupted Amy.

"And I will do my best to expedite things. And of course, I would expect that shortly after Sarah is arrested, the DA will drop all charges against Tony Capadora."

"Art, I have one favor to ask of you. I understand that Sarah has breakfast almost every day at the Lefferts Diner. On the day you plan to arrest Sarah, can you do it at the diner or as she leaves the diner and let me speak to her first, privately, at the diner?"

"No promises, but I'll see what I can do. Why do you want to speak to Sarah?"

"Art, this may not make sense to you, but I want to explain to her why I had to do what I did, putting aside the fact that I was hired to do it. I want to tell her that I feel great empathy for her in some ways but that framing Tony was totally unforgivable."

"Amy, I think that what you say makes perfect sense. You're obviously a genius as a detective, and you want the criminal brought to justice, but you also have a heart. You feel empathy. It tears at you when you have a big role in ruining the life of an otherwise good person who did a very bad thing, even though in reality, she ruined her own life. As I said, I'll try to give you the opportunity to speak to Sarah at the diner."

"Thanks, Art, that's all I can ask of you." They shook hands, and Amy exited the precinct.

At two fifty, Amy arrived at the law offices of Adams and Traybert. She had a three o'clock appointment to see Tony's attorney, Mark Traybert. She had not been impressed with Mark at their first meeting, so she expected nothing. What she got was even less than she had expected.

Mark showed up twenty-five minutes late for his meeting with Amy. He made an obviously phony excuse, and they took seats. "Amy Bell. I know I've seen you before, but I'm not sure why you came to see me."

"I've been investigating the murder of Filip Beron, in an effort to clear Tony Capadora."

"Tony who? Let me check my folder." Silence for fifteen seconds. "Oh, yes, you mean Anthony Capadora. Yes, I see he's charged with first-degree murder. And I see where three weeks ago, I asked someone I'm friendly with at the DA's office if we could agree on a plea deal to reduce Tony's sentence to twenty years, which would include the possibility of parole after serving a lot less than the full term. He said he'd get back to me if a deal is possible, but so far, I haven't heard from him.

"When and if I'm offered a deal, I will, of course, meet with Tony and explain to him why he has to accept it. Otherwise, I guess we'll go to trial, and I'll have to pound the table."

Amy was confused. "Pound the table?"

"I guess you're not familiar with the old adage which says, 'When the facts are on your side, pound the facts. When the law is on your side, pound the law. And when neither is on your side, pound the table.' So at Tony's trial, I will do a lot of table pounding." Mark laughed heartily at his own adage.

"Well, Mr. Traybert, I'm happy to inform you that it probably will not be necessary for you to pound anything. There is an excellent chance that all charges against Tony will soon be dropped. I have identified the actual killer. Her name is Sarah Dimitrov. We have obtained several of Sarah's fingerprints, and two of them match one of the prints on the murder weapon.

"I'm here to give you a heads-up on this new development. Of course, you should keep in frequent touch with Detective Oteri of the NYPD regarding the situation."

Mark was silent for a few seconds, then he smiled. "That's great news! I'm glad that at our last meeting, I was able to help you move your investigation in the right direction. If Tony is actually cleared, we'll both have good reason to be very proud of ourselves."

Amy thanked Mark for his time and ran out of the office before he could try to shake hands. She thought to herself that Mark was living proof that luck plays a big factor in success.

Over dinner, Amy updated her husband. "Jerry, I can't understand how Mark Traybert has an excellent reputation as a defense attorney."

"I suspect that years ago, he did a great job getting defendants off in a few widely publicized cases, and his reputation from those cases has stuck with him."

"That makes sense."

"Amy, why do you think Sarah didn't leave this country and return to Bulgaria immediately after killing Filip and framing Tony? She must have realized that staying here greatly increased her chances of being brought to justice."

"I'm sure it was overconfidence. She was positive that she had gotten away with the murder. And Tony had been arrested for the killing. Also, I think she likes it here. She may have a nice job, but she greatly enjoys taking off from work and being in New York for three months every couple of years."

Her husband nodded. "Makes sense. So when do you think they'll arrest Sarah for murder?"

"Art knows that time is of the essence. So I'm expecting an arrest by Monday at the latest. After all, September fifteenth is next Thursday."

Friday, September 9, 2016

At six in the evening, Amy received a phone call from Detective Oteri. She put on the speakerphone. "Amy, it's all set, we will be arresting Sarah tomorrow morning. Be at the Lefferts Diner by seven thirty and wait for Sarah to show up. We'll give you a chance to talk to her before we arrest her. But if Sarah's not there by ten thirty, or if we see her leave her house and head somewhere else, you will not get your chance."

"OK, Art, I'll be there tomorrow morning by seven thirty."

"And, Amy, we checked and discovered that Sarah is indeed booked on a Lufthansa flight to Frankfort on September fifteenth, connecting to Sofia on the sixteenth."

Amy thanked Art for calling and smiled at her husband. "Jerry, so you heard the great news! We're getting up at five thirty tomorrow morning."

"What do you mean by 'we'? Do you want me to go with you to the diner?"

"No, I guess you can go back to bed after I leave the house."

"So you want to tell Sarah you're sorry but you had to do it?"

"Not exactly, but something like that. I don't think she'd be willing to see me once she's in jail, so this is possibly my only opportunity."

Saturday, September 10, 2016

At 8:45 a.m., Sarah entered the Lefferts Diner alone and was escorted to a table. She exchanged pleasantries with several diner employees and gave her order. Then Amy walked over to Sarah's table.

"Sarah, my name is Amy. I need to speak to you." Amy didn't wait for a response. She sat down opposite Sarah, who looked confused and said nothing.

"I was hired to save Tony Capadora." Now, Sarah's expression changed to one of fear. She instantly understood. "I had to find out the truth. And I did."

Sarah glanced toward the front and the rear of the diner and saw police officers in both places.

"Sarah, 'I'll Never Believe It' is a beautiful song. I love the melody. You composed it, and Filip stole it from you. You once loved him, and then he changed. He became mean to you, and he struck you several times." Now Sarah was crying.

"It was wrong for you to shoot Filip. But I can understand the deep hurt that propelled you into doing it. However, framing Tony, an innocent man, by putting the gun in his backyard, is unforgivable. And if you hadn't framed Tony, I wouldn't have been hired, and you almost certainly would have gotten away with killing Filip.

"But as it stands, this past Wednesday, after you finished eating breakfast here and left your table, we collected two napkins and a glass from your table, and we obtained several of your fingerprints. Two of them matched a fingerprint on the murder weapon.

"So in one sense, I feel very sorry that I had to do this to you, but in another sense, I'm not sorry, because I've saved Tony from a long prison sentence."

With tears streaming down her face, Sarah spoke. "Filip took away all my self-esteem. Then he took away my song. I once loved him, and then he did all this to me. I should have been able to get over it, but I couldn't. And I know I shouldn't have done what I did to Tony. Please tell him I'm sorry. I'm not a bad person. I'm so sorry…"

At this point, two police officers approached the table and initiated the arrest process. Amy got up from her chair and exited the diner. She arrived home at eleven fifteen. Jeremy was out playing tennis; he got back at one thirty.

"So, sweetheart, did you get to speak to Sarah?"

"Yes, I got to speak my piece. Sarah was crying. She is probably, under normal circumstances, a sweet, generous, kind person. Tragically, Filip changed everything for her, for the worst."

"Well, you should be very proud that you have saved Tony. And you are the only person who could have saved him. Without you, Tony would almost surely have been sent to jail for decades, if not life."

Amy nodded. "Jerry, you're right. And I expect the charges against Tony will be dropped very shortly."

Tuesday, September 13, 2016

At eleven in the morning, Amy's office phone rang. It was Tony. "Amy, I just found out that all charges against me have been dropped! My lawyer says they have arrested a woman whose prints match one of the prints on the gun. You are responsible for all this, right?"

"Yes, you're correct; my Spy4U colleagues and I are responsible." Amy went through the details on how she identified Sarah as the killer.

"Amy, I know that Steven is paying your fees and expenses, but I essentially owe you my life. What can I do to properly thank you?"

"Tony, I will tell you what you can do to thank me, but first, let's select a mutually convenient date for my husband, Jerry, and me to take you and Steven out to dinner, our treat. After what you've been put though, you sure as hell deserve it. And Steven deserves it because he had faith all along in your innocence.

"Now as to what you can do. You wrote a beautiful song, 'It's Not in My Power.' I love listening to it, and lots of other people do too. I want you to continue to write beautiful songs, giving so many people, including me, the great pleasure of listening to them.

"I have an appointment tomorrow to meet with Morton Glassberg, the head of Acme Melodies, which recorded Filip's songs. I'll explain to him why it's in his best interest to publicly announce that you are the true composer of 'It's Not in My Power.'

"In addition to Morton getting you paid your appropriate royalties, I want him to commit himself to seriously listening to all the songs you have composed that you will present to him and to giving you any constructive advice he can to enable you to improve your songwriting skills.

"So I'll phone you, probably tomorrow, and tell you how things went at Acme. But one way or another, the best way you can thank me is by continuing to compose songs."

"Amy, thank you again, for everything. I'm looking forward to our dinner. And I will definitely keep writing songs."

Amy said goodbye and then phoned her husband. "Jerry, the charges against Tony have been dropped."

"Fantastic!"

"And we're gonna treat Tony and Steven to a celebratory dinner. How about at Big Tony's? I'm getting fonder and fonder of that place."

"Fine with me."

"OK, I'll work it out with them. I told Tony that the best way for him to thank me is to keep writing songs."

"Well, if Tony can compose more songs like 'It's Not in My Power,' he'll have a new career for himself as a songwriter."

"That's true, Jerry. And along those lines, I'm seeing Morton at the Acme building tomorrow to persuade him to do the right thing with regard to getting Tony the royalties and respect he deserves."

"Sweetheart, if Morton is a decent man, you shouldn't have to work too hard to convince him to do the right thing for Tony."

"You're sure as hell right about that. Also, how about we go see Blake's play, *Very Valuable*, this Sunday afternoon?"

"You mean the play that earned you ten thousand dollars? Sure, why not?" They both laughed.

Jeremy changed the subject. "Do you think you'll receive a bonus for solving Filip's murder and getting the killer arrested?"

"Yes, Jerry, I do. In the murder case where I first met Steven, he was the client, as he is now. For this type of case, if there is a bonus, I split the money fifty-fifty with Spy4U. And in that first case, my half of the bonus was twenty thousand dollars."

"Wow!" exclaimed Jeremy. "I think I do now remember that amount."

"So if I had to guess, I would predict I'll receive another twenty thousand for solving this case. But I never count my chickens;

I let Mr. Murray count them for me and negotiate the best deal he can. Steven is worth several million, so he can indeed be generous if he wants to reward me."

"But," her husband pointed out, with a sly smile on his face—which was, of course, not visible to his wife over the phone—"Steven is probably not as wealthy as Anita will be, when she turns twenty-one. By the way, is Steven married?"

"No, he's a widower."

Now Jeremy's smile became bigger and slyer. "I wonder, could Steven possibly be viewed as a celebrity? Because if so, you could give him—"

"Shame on you," interrupted Amy, who was definitely not pleased. "You are a bad boy with a dirty, dirty mind!"

"Shucks, sweetheart, I just want your clients to be as satisfied as possible." He then broke out into hysterical and uncontrollable laughter. Amy listened to this outburst for about ten seconds and then hung up.

Wednesday, September 14, 2016

Amy arrived home at 5:20 p.m. and hugged and kissed her husband. "I met with Morton and Barry at Acme. They were very interested in all the details of how I solved the case. And they were very embarrassed when I pointed out that since all of Filip's other song compositions were lousy, they should have been much more suspicious as to who really wrote his two hit songs.

"Anyhow, Morton readily agreed to all my suggestions. He'll make sure that Tony gets all the royalties he deserves. He'll publicize the fact that Tony is the true composer of 'It's Not in My Power.' He'll listen to any songs Tony brings to him, and he'll get the appropriate Acme person to also listen and to give Tony some advice on how to improve his song composing."

Jeremy was contemplative. "You know, this whole case is a tragedy of people brought down by personality problems they couldn't get under control.

"Filip had a beautiful and wealthy girlfriend who was crazy about him and who, over time, probably would have composed many beautiful songs for him to record and perform. But then he threw it all away because he couldn't control his impulse to change his behavior with girlfriends from love and kindness to meanness and physical violence.

"And Sarah couldn't get over what Filip had done to her. She couldn't put it aside and move ahead with her privileged life in Sofia. Instead, she became more and more hateful toward Filip and generally miserable."

"You got that right. And Denise will be happy to hear that her advice helped me solve the case. You know, if she didn't happen to be studying Russian, it's very possible that Sarah would have gotten away with murder; isn't that amazing?"

Her husband nodded. "Yes, and Tony was the victim of an awful coincidence—namely, that the Cyrillic letters spelling out 'Sarah' that Filip wrote out as he died happened to be, in English, the first four letters of Tony's last name."

"That's certainly true. By the way, Jerry, you basically gave me the solution to the whole case way back on the first day. You told me I should listen to Tony's other songs. If they were all lousy, then I could assume that Tony did not compose 'It's Not in My Power.'

"All I had to do was change 'Tony' to 'Filip' in what you said and also change 'It's Not in My Power' to 'I'll Never Believe It.' Then I would have realized pretty quickly that Filip probably stole his first hit song from somebody in Bulgaria, and I might have been able to solve the case in a couple of days. But instead, I made fun of you and told you I didn't have to listen to Tony's songs, because Franklin could ask him on the polygraph whether he wrote 'It's Not in My Power.'

"Because you are were so handsome and sexy, I didn't realize how incredibly perceptive you can also be—sometimes." Her husband laughed.

"Now, Jerry, I have an Occam's razor problem for you. Given that an hour from now, all your current tension will be relieved, and I will have a very satisfied smile on my face, what is Occam's least complex explanation?"

Jeremy had very little difficulty figuring out the solution. He said nothing, but he grabbed Amy by the rear end and guided her into the bedroom. Dinner would have to wait.

The End

About the Author

David Schwinger is retired, having spent his entire career teaching mathematics at City College, City University of New York. He now lives in Florida with his wife, Sherryl, whom he met when she was his student.

In addition to having written eleven Amy Bell murder mysteries, David composes songs and plays table tennis and pickleball. He and Sherryl have traveled to over 130 countries.

David began his mystery-writing career in 2013, upon the urging of his wife. *The Teacher's Pet Murders*, his first book, was inspired by the secret romantic relationship David had with Sherryl while she was his student at City College. In that book, his vivacious and brilliant heroine/detective, Amy Bell, made her first appearance. Amy has continued to use her extraordinary talents to solve murders in all of David's succeeding books.

CPSIA information can be obtained
at www.ICGtesting.com
Printed in the USA
LVHW040107211020
669276LV00004B/369